TWO DOCTORS
AND A GIRL

Elizabeth Seifert

Thorndike Press • **Chivers Press**
Thorndike, Maine USA Bath, England

MID-CONTINENT PUBLIC LIBRARY
South Independence Branch
13700 E. 35th St.
Independence, MO 64055

SI

This Large Print edition is published by Thorndike Press, USA and by Chivers Press, England.

Published in 1999 in the U.S. by arrangement with Spectrum Literary Agency.

Published in 1999 in the U.K. by arrangement with Ralph M. Vicinanza Ltd.

U.S. Hardcover 0-7862-1763-4 (Candlelight Series Edition)
U.K. Hardcover 0-7540-3675-8 (Chivers Large Print)
U.K. Softcover 0-7540-3676-6 (Camden Large Print)

The text of this Large Print edition is unabridged. Other aspects of the book may vary from the original edition.

Set in 16 pt. Plantin by Minnie B. Raven.

Printed in the United States on permanent paper.

British Library Cataloguing in Publication Data available

Library of Congress Cataloging in Publication Data

Seifert, Elizabeth, 1897–
    Two doctors and a girl / by Elizabeth Seifert.
        p.   cm.
    ISBN 0-7862-1763-4 (lg. print : hc : alk. paper)
    1. Physicians — Middle West — Family relationships —
Fiction.   2. Large type books.   I. Title.
[PS3537.E352T88   1999]
    813'.52—dc21
                                                        98-49037

TWO DOCTORS
AND A GIRL

TWO DOCTORS
AND A GIRL

Chapter 1

"Out here on the beach, early morning is really beautiful," said Tim Dineen, turning reluctantly away from the wide window, back to the conference room and the table surrounded by almost the entire medical staff of the hospital. Consultant to that hospital, the surgeon knew the staff members well — their skills, their lack of skill, their achievements, their failures.

"I myself admire the beach *and* the ocean more with the sun risen and shining down upon it," growled one of the white-jacketed men.

Tim nodded. "Seven is early for anyone," he agreed. "And if the program I am about to offer you is any good, perhaps it will show us how to avoid these early-bird meetings. Now! Let's get to it!"

He was a large man, Dr. Dineen. Tall, broad-shouldered. A surgeon, Chief of Orthopedic Services at the large teaching hospital in the city thirty miles inland from the beach, this resort, this hospital and its staff. Still less than forty, he was one of those men who look mature at thirty, and who do not change very much in his second thirty years. His skin was a healthy brown, his black hair close-cropped. He was a very masculine man, whose nose dominated his chin. Some called him handsome.

This was a good hospital, well-staffed, and small only in relation to the complex of buildings and services in the city where Tim worked. Its staff was entirely competent, many of them young, and several older than Tim Dineen. They all listened respectfully to what he had to say about their participation in a project of the Medical Association in which he believed. Eric Ritter, Senior Resident, had suggested that he address the staff on the subject. Qualified himself to become a senior staff member, he had his ideals and ideas about what a staff of doctors should be.

Tim spoke crisply, without pressure. He believed in continuing education for all doctors, beginners as well as those qualified. He mentioned the three states that required such additional training, he discussed the quickly changing medical picture, citing burn treatment, heart monitoring as examples. "It's a slippery business, the medical knowledge we thought we'd stowed into our little black bags when we picked up our

M.D.'s. I am not asking or advising you to take a stand on the State's requirement of this training. You can guess how I feel. But I am going to mention to you the questionnaire being offered by the American Medical Association — you'll get one — and based on the fact that that same association has been offering you nine hours of concentrated studies each year resulting in certificates of continuing education. I won't suggest that you doctors believe that the older, more experienced doctors have more knowledge than the others. All of us can guess that the longer a medic is out of school, the more obsolete his information becomes. That happens pretty fast unless the M.D. we're talking about works in a teaching hospital or a medical school. Even if he does, some of the more sophisticated advances are difficult for him to keep track of.

"So! Three states have set up programs insuring the continuing education of their accredited doctors. Recently Federal laws have required the regular review of medics to continue their accreditation. But these laws are hard to implement, and an effort is being made to set up this continuing education. These questionnaires have been prepared to set up a system of self-examination. There are seven hundred and fifty questions —"

A groan rumbled around the table. Tim's hand brushed back across his hair. "I know," he conceded. "I too am bogged down in paper work. But these questions do deserve, say, a weekend of concentration and answering. They are designed to test an M.D.'s knowledge of the most recent tested treatment regimens. So far, twelve thousand surgeons have applied for the tests. The A.M.A. wants more. These questionnaires are mailed out by a bonding company so that no one will know who has applied. The results are computerized, and the results will not be made public. The Board will know how many people missed each question, they'll know by specialty how each doctor does, and they have already confirmed that the longer a doctor is out of school, the more education he needs.

"I am prepared to answer one question from you. Have I filled out the packet of questions? Yes, I have. I believe it can't hurt me, and I am hoping it will help. Thank you."

He sat down, he stood again — talk swept the room. A telephone summons came for Dr. Ritter, and he left. Tim's dark eyes watched the young man go. Other matters came up, he began to look at his wristwatch, but took minutes to say to those near him that Ritter was doing a fine job. "He should have done well on his Board exams."

The doctors near him at the table added their words of praise for young Dr. Ritter. He was, said Dr. Childers, O.B.-Gyn., the finest surgical resident he, personally, had ever known.

"He should go far," Dr. Dineen agreed, murmuring *thank you* to the man who had set a fresh cup of coffee before him. "In surgery or research. Do you know his plans?"

"He's taken the Board exams," said the man across the table. "This past week, I think."

"He was rather young . . ." said Tim.

"He'll pass. And there's a big position available to him if he gets his diplomate."

Dr. Dineen nodded. "He *is* young for that!" he affirmed his previous statement.

Before his eyes rose the picture of "young" Dr. Ritter, who was, indeed, young. Thirty at the most. A serious, sturdy young man with thick, smooth blond hair, a thoughtful young face. And he was a good doctor as well, having escaped the temptations and handicaps of a young man born into a very rich, a very prominent family. He had fairly won the praise he was getting this morning.

"He should at least have tried for the diplomate," Tim agreed, "if the job is worthwhile."

"Eric thinks it is. It is in England."

"Where they have National medicine."

"Yes. But they have begun to recognize their difficulties with research, and are setting up programs. Eric thinks some fine opportunities are offered."

"And he wants to upgrade his research program," another voice contributed. "He's sure to pass the Board."

The Chief of Staff resumed charge of the meeting, and the talk subsided. Reports were made, discussion freshened. Tim was used to being asked to share in these meetings; he was a staff consultant. When favors were asked of him, he was as generous as his own affairs would allow him to be. He liked the staff men, he was friends with many of them.

Breakfast was brought in, grapefruit, sweet rolls and coffee, and he could share the relaxed talk about girls, the beach, and the fine hotel which the Ritter family owned and had made popular. Its success, Tim had decided, was due to the excellent service always available. He seldom passed up a chance to say this to the local residents.

"That, and the good beach," agreed his neighbor that morning. There was a twinkle in his eye. He knew Tim quite well.

"It is a good beach," Dr. Dineen agreed. "Especially the part of it owned and controlled by the hotel. They keep it clean, and in as natural a state as is possible."

Again his mind's eye wandered. The beach was a fine one, a wide expanse of smooth sand and tidal flats as silvery as the ocean itself. There was a minimum of cabanas and umbrellas; commercial projects were not allowed at all, no signboards, no hot dog stands or pop machines. This kept litter at a minimum, too, which lately made the previously unwelcome restriction better accepted. Young and old, guests of the hotel were allowed to entertain themselves, to swim, to play, to sunbathe on that stretch of smooth brown sand. Even the lifeguard towers, tall and slender, were unobtrusive. The tidal flats afforded wealth for shell seekers. It was a pleasant, peaceful place, of the sort that was, each year, getting to be more rare and treasured.

"I heard a girl say that your beach here was like walking on moonstones," said Tim, with an apologetic smile.

"Sounds like Gayle Colburn," said one of the younger men, his eyes brightening.

It had been Gayle's sister, but Tim said nothing. Again he looked at his watch "If there are no further surgical problems," he suggested to the Chief.

"There are the tissue reports," Dr. Curren reminded him.

Tim settled back in his chair. He wanted to go back to the hotel, where he had left his car the afternoon before. He wanted to look in on Amy again, and then drive the thirty miles back to the city, and there take up his full schedule at the hospital complex. Amy would not care if he came back to see her or not. He made these trips regularly; he took good care of Amy.

Poor thing. Mental pictures came again, swiftly, flipping over, one on top of the other. Amy. His wife. His "bride," really. Of ten years. His memory pictures were all too swift, too few. She was an invalid now, and had been for years. The words to be said of such a situation were repellent to him. He "kept" Amy at the hotel, she and her nurse. The nurses changed, Amy did not.

The hotel — it was not a sanitarium. Definitely not that. But many people stayed there, or lived there, because of the good air, the quiet, and always the service. In addition, Dr. Dineen had his work at the hospital only thirty miles away. Amy could be left with a clear conscience; the nurses, and the hotel, even the Peter's Beach Hospital, would care for her in her husband's absence. It was good for the work he did, to be sure of that.

The breakfast was now being cleared away, and papers were again drawn forward. Conscious of his brief silence, Tim turned to his neighbor. "The British have taken over the hotel, you know," he said.

"The . . . ?"

"Yes. It seems there's a training ship anchored in the neighborhood."

"Oh, yes. There was a dance, I believe —"

"And no Paul Revere to warn you."

"Did we need one?" Dr. Barker was white-moustached, and not too interested in foreign navies and a hotel dance.

"Couldn't you find a bed?" asked the man across from them.

"Oh, yes," said Tim. "But it was rather startling, to come in unprepared. The band, the officers and the men, were everywhere. Evidently they were forming up for a parade."

"Mhmmmn. Full dress. Marched through the hospital grounds. The kids loved it."

"And most of the adults, female," growled the Gynecologist.

Tim chuckled. "You can't beat a uni-

15

form," he agreed. "They certainly have taken over the hotel. Even the bellhops — and the doorman — they all have new uniforms of red coats and light blue trousers. And enough gold braid to dazzle anyone. And if you think *those* uniforms have not taken over Ritter's, you simply do not know the hotel and those bellhops! Me in my sports coat and polyester slacks got smuggled out the back door, even in the early morning."

The Pathologist was standing and rattling the papers in his hand. The Chief of Staff rapped for attention. Order was restored. Tim sat half-turned from the table and let his thoughts go back to the hotel and the uniformed men, to Nancy Colburn, with whom he had watched the fun the evening before.

If any tissue report demanded his attention, that attention would be given.

Nancy had worn a red and white striped dress, a red scarf confining her yellow hair which frequently had to be tucked back. She had come to the hotel, maybe to watch the sailors. She had warmly greeted Dr. Dineen, and had said, yes, she was enjoying her vacation, and then turned again to watch the people on the wide terrace and inside the wide and handsome lobby of the hotel.

Nancy, as sweet and pretty a girl as one would find anywhere. She worked for Tim, with Tim, back at the hospital.

He had known her, had known all the Colburns, ever since he had begun making his regular trips to the Beach. It had been Tim who suggested to Nancy that she train as a surgical assistant, at the time a new branch of nursing. He had taken an unfailing interest in that training, and now she was well-established in a good profession. She was popular in the hospital complex, and in demand by surgeons other than Dr. Dineen. In the Beach Hospital too, Tim suspected. If Gayle where not already here, Nancy might think she should work here, and so be near her parents.

But Gayle definitely was here! She ran a shop at the hotel, but she lived at home. She was a great girl, older than Nancy, prettier perhaps — really a dazzling young woman, full of life and enthusiasm.

Amy said that Nancy was good to her. She never had mentioned Gayle, and Tim was not sure that Gayle had ever gone up to her rooms.

The tissue reports were taking too long, and Tim whispered to his neighbor that he would have to leave; he would return in a week. And he did leave, with eyes following him. What were those eyes seeing, what were the minds thinking as he left? It was the sort of speculation in which Tim frequently indulged; he was deeply interested in people, all people, and in their impact on each other.

So he went along the hospital corridor, told the operator that he was leaving — he would be back at the Center by ten. The operator, too, watched him go.

Tall, dark, well-dressed in his small-checked coat over a dark red shirt, he walked with authority, saw everything before him, but his thoughts probed into his memory and knowledge of the people who meant Peter's Beach to him.

He thought about the telephone call which had taken Eric from the meeting. Was it something special? A report on the results of the Board exams, perhaps? Or just a routine call within the hospital to the Chief Surgical Resident? Always there was an itchy feeling that such a call could involve Tim — and Amy. He thought about his arrival at the Beach the evening before, with the sailors, the gaiety — and Gayle. The lobby was crowded, and he had cut through a side hall, out to a shadowy walkway that would lead to stairs and . . .

And which also led to Gayle Colburn, a

pert yellow cap back on her dark head, a yellow and white striped shirt-thing, and slacks of some nondescript color — the shadows were deep and wavering because of the blowing trees.

She was sitting on the stucco rail of the passageway, a flowering tree behind her, its top highlighted by the setting sun. In that glow he could quite plainly see Gayle's vivid face, her brilliant smile, hear her clear, intense voice.

She was looking up at, talking to, smiling at, a man. Tim did not know him. He was not one of the sailors, he may have worked at the hotel, or been a guest — it didn't matter who he was. He was tall, young, very handsome, his pullover sweater was ribbed cashmere. He seemed charmed by Gayle, and she seemed —

Seemed. Tim had walked past the couple. "Oh, hi, Tim!" Gayle had said. The man didn't notice him. He was entranced by Gayle. As many men, perhaps all men, were entranced by that girl. Even Tim, in his time.

Gayle. And Nancy. Sisters, and as unlike as two girls could possibly be. Even Tim could not say which was "better." Blonde hair or dark? A gentle glow against a blinding spotlight? A bubbling laugh, a friendly voice

19

against excitement and challenge?

When he reached the hotel drive, Tim looked again at his watch and decided that he would not "bother" Amy again. It really made no difference. And he went on to his car, still thinking. He wished Nancy was with him, ending her vacation. But of course she was not. She still had the weekend and a couple of extra days. He settled into the car seat, trying to concentrate on the work ahead of him. He would do surgery at three, but, beginning at ten, there would be conferences, rounds, new patients to see . . .

Parallel with this line of thought was a summary of the past eighteen hours. Just as, a good driver, he could watch the road ahead and be also aware of the one behind him, of the beach he was leaving, and the gentle, purring waves that curled brightly upon it. A man on the beach crossed his line of vision. Tim might know him, he might not. He could be the man with whom Gayle had flirted the night before. *Flirted* was an outmoded word. Each generation of young people always searched for and used expressive terms. He could think of a whole procession of such words, all meaning the same thing. Did girls now "make out" instead of "flirt"? Or was *make out* something heavier?

Heavy. While scrubbing, he had heard the

chattering young nurses in o.r. speak of matters as being *heavy* between a man and a girl. Any girl. Any man.

Gayle. Gayle flirted. And sometimes she allowed things to become "heavy." Not always. Not even often. But always she flirted.

Late yesterday when Tim had left Nancy after watching the parade and had gone down to the beach, Gayle had been there, doing acrobatics with some young man. Both had worn slacks and pullover sweaters. The man was not the same one of the shadowy passageway that night at sunset. This chap was younger. Redheaded. And quite an athlete. He had held Gayle on his shoulders and marched with her along the sand, keeping step with the music from the naval band. He had jogged along the edge of the retreating tide, threatening to dump Gayle in the water. He had done splits, with her still on his shoulders, laughing, squealing — the man shouted with youthful exuberance.

Tim had walked on down the beach, stooping to pick up a sand dollar, aware still of the music up at the hotel, seeing everything, but resting his mind, deliberately lapsing into a state of semi-consciousness which was as restful as sleep would have been.

It was something of a shock to feel her hand on his arm, to hear her clear voice speak his name.

"Tim Dineen, will you stop making me slog through this blasted sand?"

"Gayle . . ." he had said helplessly.

The clogs she wore — Yes, they would slog through sand. The heels must be four inches high.

She sat down like a child and emptied the silly things. She patted the sand beside her, smiling up at him. "Let's talk," she said.

He did sit down, drawing up his knees, clasping his hands around them. He watched the ocean, listened to its voice. Gulls flew low to inspect the people, a sandpiper ran along the glistening water edge.

Gayle replaced her shoes and dusted her hands, shook her thick hair back from her face. "You passed me and didn't speak," she said. "I had to run, and run . . ."

"You didn't seem to be lonesome."

She stared at him. "Oh!" she said. "Muscle man."

"He could have broken your back, tossing you around."

"But he didn't."

"Were you having fun?"

She shrugged. "I guess so. Would you have — ?"

"A cigarette! No."

"Mr. Clean," she murmured. "I know."

Tim watched the gulls ride the waves.

"Did you come down here to see me?" she asked.

"To the beach?"

"Well, down here."

"No," he said. "I often come down."

"I know. Every ten days."

"I try to make it about that often."

"But not to see me." Her eyes were bright, her smile challenging.

He said nothing.

"I've known you to come for that reason," she murmured "And I keep hoping . . ."

"Don't be silly."

"I'm not. I'm just in love with a man who won't admit that I am."

He should have gotten up then and left her. He did turn to look back at the hotel. "They are having a great time back there," he said.

"Oh, they are," she agreed, her tone dry. "That's why we closed the boutique. Nobody sees or buys anything, not with sailors to watch."

"I'd think you'd watch them."

"I did, for a time. I went to the dance last night. It was fun. Got a little rowdy, of course."

"And you didn't like that."

"Well, of course I liked it. But I knew you wouldn't . . ."

"Are you calling me stodgy, by any means?"

She laughed at his tone of pretended affront. She put her hand on his arm. "No, of course not, darling. I know you too well. You're really a beautiful man."

He laughed.

"But you are, Tim! Sometimes your profession makes you a little stiff —"

"I have a reputation to take care of."

"Oh, I *know!*" She had spoken with the tremendous exaggeration which, for him, was such an exciting part of this handsome, outward-going girl. She loved people, she wanted them to love her. There was no put-on with Gayle. She had a way of setting goals for herself, and reaching them. But . . .

"I didn't stay up at the hotel with the navy," she said now. "I knew you had come in this afternoon —"

"Nancy told you?"

"Mother told me. Nancy's probably been watching the parade."

"Perhaps we should go up and see what's going on now."

Her hand firmly held his arm "No," she said. "I want to talk. Me to you, and you to me. The way you used to talk to me."

"Oh, Gayle . . ."

"I know. You said we had to grow up."

"You. Not me. I've been grown-up for years."

"I know. Old man Tim. But I still love you. You know that I do."

"Gayle —"

"You know that I do!" she insisted.

"I told you . . ."

"I know what you told me. To find another man."

Yes, he had told her that.

"But there aren't any other men, Tim. Not like you."

"Which may be a hopeful sign for the world."

"Don't get smarty. I'm trying to have a serious talk with you. I do love you . . ."

"And you do something else. You keep forgetting why I broke off with you in the first place."

She no longer was touching him. She even looked away from him, and pretended to be interested in the little round cups of sand she was scooping and molding. "Amy," she said, like a sulking child.

"Yes, Amy."

"But why?" she asked, turning fiercely to look at him. "That summer — when you first came here — you loved me!"

"I made love to you. There's a difference. And it was wrong —"

"It was wonderful. And you know it."

It had, indeed, been wonderful. Seven years ago. Gayle was eighteen. He was a resident surgeon, and not yet skilled in a life without a wife, without a girl.

For six weeks, yes, it had been wonderful. Their meetings, their swift, hot embraces, the times she had come to the city, the times he had come down here to see Amy, and to be with Gayle.

For six weeks it had been madness. Nothing but madness could come of it. He had been the older one, the wiser one.

"I told you then, Gayle," he said soberly, "I tell you now, that you would do better to find a man with whom you'd have a chance to build a good life."

"You said it would be sensible. That's what you said."

"It was sensible."

"But not *better*, Tim, darling."

He stood up. "It was all we could have."

"It was enough. It would be enough now."

"Oh, Gayle, for Pete's sake! I told you to find another man, and there must have been dozens of them in all the years."

She looked up at him, her hazel eyes clear.

"I don't sleep with dozens of men, Tim."

Instantly he was contrite. "I'm sorry," he said quickly. "I know you don't."

The minute was gone. "How do you know?" she asked boldly.

He laughed, relieved to have the mood changed. "Don't get sassy with me," he advised. "Nancy says —"

"She's up there on the terrace now, watching us."

Tim had seen her. A small figure in her red and white dress. "She's not *watching* us!" he assured Gayle.

She shrugged. "It would make no difference if she were. Tim Dineen is always a perfect gentleman."

He decided to ignore the barb and the chance she had given him to answer, to argue —

"When Nancy speaks of you, Gayle," he said, "she couples your name with Eric's."

Again she shrugged. "It's been announced that I am marrying Eric," she admitted.

"You could not do better."

She glanced up. "Oh, yes, I could," she said softly.

"Listen to me! Eric is a fine fellow. He's smart, and he will go far as a doctor. In spite of the family's money, he has worked hard

27

and honestly in medicine. Not many rich men's sons would do that."

"I know Eric is a shining knight in silver armor. Every girl who knows him or meets him would agree with you."

"And he asked you to marry him."

Her eyes widened. "Of course," she said innocently. "Don't they all?" Then she flushed. "No," she corrected herself. "Not all."

"You two could make a good life together."

"And it would be the sensible thing to do."

His eyes searched the terrace. Nancy was gone. "Yes," he agreed. "It would be the sensible thing."

"There's one hitch," she said.

He waited. She was busy again with her sand sculpture. "Eric thinks I love you."

Tim jumped to his feet. "Then do the sensible thing," he said, "and tell him that you do not."

"But, Tim —"

"It would be the right thing to do, Gayle. If you plan to marry the man, start things right. You can. You can make him believe you. And I do hope that you would keep on doing just that! Will you promise to tell him that your crush on me, your affair with me, was over years ago, and that you've grown up since?"

"It was an affair," she said soberly.

"No, dear, it never was. Not really."

"But, Tim, I remember . . ."

"It was an interlude. The beach, the moonlight, two young people. I was getting over Amy's terrible accident; you were at the age for excited crushes . . ."

"It was wonderful."

"At the time it seemed to be. But it quickly was over, Gayle. And seven years ago!"

"I still love you."

He started up the beach, and she followed him. He glanced back at her. "In a way," he said slowly, "I love you, too. Much in the way I have loved Nancy, and still love her."

"Mhmmmnh," she agreed. "I remember Nancy; she fell for you, too. She was — what? — fifteen. Your tragic story was fascinating to a girl that age. You were able to seduce her into studying nursing and training to be whatever it is she has become —"

"A surgical assistant. It is a fine profession."

"And she's built a good life for herself," drawled Gayle. "In your own way, you've fixed us both up into nice, good lives."

Tim frowned and bent over to brush sand from his slacks.

"You do make it easier," Gayle told him, "to tell Eric that I am no longer in love with you!" She started to run ahead of him. "In fact," she called over her shoulder, "I'm pretty sure I hate you for it. And if Nancy has any sense —"

He could no longer hear her.

He supposed that, later that night, she had told Eric the truth about her brief "interlude" with Tim, and that she was sure it was over. Where and how she did this, he didn't care to know.

He settled down to the business of driving. The beach no longer was to be seen behind him; traffic was multiplying with each mile; the city's outskirts were about him, the city's skyline ahead. And the hospital Center.

Gayle had seen Eric on the evening before. They had had a dinner date, but some emergency had tied him up at the hospital. She supposed someone had got trampled during the parade. The mobs had been simply *awful!* He laughed and said it wasn't that kind of emergency. But she'd better eat her dinner — he'd get something —

"Between bandages," she had said. "I know —"

She said she would meet him in the walkway — where Tim saw her — some man had been ready to entertain her. Tim had seen him doing *that!*

But, finally, Eric showed up, all scrubbed and clean, wearing a light blue jacket, with a dark blue scarf at the throat. He kissed Gayle and asked if there was another chair —

"There's sure to be. Have you eaten?"

"Dinner, you mean? Did you?"

"Oh, yes. I went home for an hour. Nancy's home, you know. She came back here with me. I suppose she's around somewhere."

"Maybe we can find her." His eyes brightened. He liked Nancy. Well, almost everyone liked the girl. Females as well as the men and boys.

"I want to talk," Gayle told him. "Let's pick up a sandwich for you, some shakes, and go down to the beach." This they did, though it took quite a time, for many people stopped to speak to Eric; Gayle enjoyed watching some nonsense a group of the sailors were performing, singing and dancing a sort of jig. But finally, as the hour grew later, the older people began to leave the lobby, and she and Eric took the bag of sandwiches and their tall cups down across the terrace to the beach, deserted except for couples like themselves who, Gayle pointed out, also wanted to be alone.

"Is that what we want?" Eric teased her.

"Well, sure. Or don't we?"

"I could be alone with you in my car."

"Oh, *Doctor!*"

Tim, she supposed, was back in his precious hospital and thinking about her, wondering if she was keeping her promise to talk to Eric. Well, she was talking. Watching Eric eat his sandwich and drink some of the shake which was not as cold nor as good as it would have been a half hour earlier. He could drink hers, too. She didn't want it.

They talked about the sailors, they talked about Nancy's two-week vacation . . .

"I should have put her to work," said Eric. "We don't enjoy the luxury of surgical assistants."

It was Eric's idea of "talk;" it might have been Tim's. But Gayle was pretty sure it was what he had meant when he asked — ordered? — insisted! — that she tell Eric the truth about herself and Tim. He had said it would give her her only chance with Eric, with Tim, and with herself. Whatever that could have meant. It evidently did mean a lot to Tim. There were tines when he "made her sick!" There had been times when, very briefly, she hated him.

But if she were to be, quote, entirely honest, unquote — She had been that when, this afternoon, she had told him that she still loved him. Because she did.

Seven years ago, for six weeks, Amy had made no difference. Now, she still need make no difference. But Tim couldn't see that. He had listened to Gayle's declaration, her confession of love, and he had walked away from her. If she could think that he, too, wished . . .

He didn't. He had told her —

And now she was about to do as he had said, talk to Eric, and tell him . . .

There were many ways to do this. "Be honest." Tim's way. And —

Two of the romantic couples had left the beach. Up at the hotel, the crowd had noticeably thinned. The ocean lapped against this sheltered arc of sand, whispering as the waters rolled in and dissolved.

"Eric," said Gayle, drawing her knees up to her chin, "were you here in the hospital when Tim Dineen brought his wife to the hotel?"

"Oh, gracious!" he cried. "I don't remember. But I don't think so. How long ago was that, Gayle?"

"Seven years. I was thinking about it this

afternoon. He had come down for one of his visits."

"Well, let's see. Four years, two — that's six! No. Seven years ago I was a senior medic."

"Still in college?"

"Well, in med school. Yes! That's right. Dineen had come on staff at the teaching hospital. We liked him. He was — he *is* — a fine teacher."

"I liked him, too," said Gayle softly.

So softly that Eric looked sharply at her. "What do you mean by that?" he asked.

"Oh, it seemed very romantic, and sad, and thrilling — all at once. His wife being so sick, and he such a young and handsome doctor. Every girl around was ready to sympathize with him, and make up for his tragedy."

"Even you."

"Well, of course. I was eighteen."

"Yes. I remember."

"Oh, you do not!"

"I do! You were so pretty, and exciting. But of course, just then, my main excitement was about getting my M.D. and being an intern."

"It still is your main excitement, isn't it?" she asked, her tone light.

"Well, not excitement, really. But —" He

34

reached for her hand. "You understand this," he told her. "I'm sure you know that I am the sort of doctor who thinks always of his profession, who believes that profession must come first in his life."

"You bet I know that," said Gayle vigorously. "That's why I ate dinner alone this evening."

"Without me, you mean. I know that you did, and I am sorry. But that's just the way it is."

"And we've talked it all out before," she said.

"Yes, we have. I'd like to think you understood about the frustrations . . ."

Her head lifted. "What frustrations?" she asked.

"Tonight I would have rather been with you."

"Honestly?" She was surprised.

He laughed. "Honestly," he agreed.

"Do you suppose Tim Dineen . . . ?"

"Lordy, Gayle, that man is a bundle of frustrations. I hope his work satisfies him somewhat. But his wife —"

"Amy."

"Yes, Amy. Think what it must be to have his young wife a total invalid . . . Do you know her?"

"I've seen her. When she first came here,

she'd be out in a wheelchair. But lately . . . no-o." She broke off. "Hmmmmn . . ."

He touched her shoulder. "What is it, darling?"

"I was thinking about the frustration thing. I suppose it would explain — for Tim, at least . . ."

He was watching her closely. "Explain what, Gayle?"

She glanced at him. "Oh, nothing," she said.

"Not *nothing*. That's no answer to give me, sweetheart."

She rubbed her cheek against his shoulder. "It's been over for so long," she murmured.

"What's been over?"

"My crush on Tim." She laughed a little. "I called it an affair. Can you imagine?"

"Seven years ago?"

"Yes. I was sorry for him, of course. I was sure he was lonely —"

"Was it an affair?" There was a thin edge to his voice.

"The word has so many meanings. I had this crush on Tim. Then, when he recognized that I did, he would have made something of it. But I was young, and not ready for anything of the sort. Afterward, I suppose when he admitted that he would get no-

36

where with me — we'd stayed good friends, of course. But then was when he began to notice Nancy. She's really lovely, Eric."

"Yes, she is. A very pretty girl, sweet and friendly. She always has been."

"You remember us both as we were several years ago. Six, five — Nancy at fifteen, seventeen, and eighteen. Just a kid. I can't help but decide, excusing all of Tim's frustrations, that it was a dreadful thing for him to do to a child."

"Oh, now, Gayle . . ."

"He took her from the shelter of our home. She works with him; she would be the first to say she adores him. But what can come of that adoration?"

He drew her close and kissed her. She almost nodded with her satisfaction. Yes, she knew Eric. She could count on him to be loyal to injured womanhood.

"Don't blame Tim," she whispered into his ear.

He kissed her again. "I love you, Gayle," he said earnestly. "You are so beautiful; you excite me. You and my work together — you are my whole life, my future."

She drew back to look into his eyes. Then she put her hands on his cheeks and drew him toward her. "Sometimes, Eric," she said, "I mean what I say."

"I think I know the times. And they are wonderful. I love you for them."

"I know you do. You are a sweet and honest man."

"Well, yes — maybe. Now! This sand is getting damp. Let's go up."

"To bed."

He smiled at her. "For now," he said, "I'll take you home, then go back to the hospital."

"And think about me?"

"I'm afraid so."

They gathered up the sandwich bag, the napkins, and the shake cups. And they started up the slope to the hotel. Gayle put her hand through Eric's arm. He smiled at her.

"I suppose you know," she said, "that I wouldn't marry you except for your money."

He chuckled and pressed her hand warmly against his side. "I told you I knew when you meant what you were saying."

She nodded. "I'll have to be careful, won't I?"

Nancy had seen Tim down on the beach with Gayle. She had spent the early part of the afternoon at home, talking to her mother, sampling a new cookie, still warm from the oven. She had picked three blooms from her father's rosebushes, smelling each one to be sure it had perfume, and then she said she was going down to the hotel to see Amy.

This was not unusual. She often went to see Amy when she came to the Beach; she had frequently seen her this time when she was home on vacation.

Her mother mentioned the sailors.

"Oh, I'll look at them, too," Nancy promised, running down the walk, her red and white skirt blowing in the soft breeze, her twist of golden hair swinging against her shoulders.

Mrs. Colburn smiled. Nancy was a *nice* girl, she told herself. Such problems as she had were those of any girl entering full womanhood. It was — restful — to be around Nancy.

The hotel was almost as familiar to Nancy as was her own home. Even on such a busy, crowded day, nearly everyone greeted her. From his tall-backed chair in the lobby, Eric's grandfather smiled and waved to her. Nancy went to him and pressed her sun-warmed cheek against his old one.

"Did you bring me flowers, darling?" he asked.

"Oh, no, Grampa. These are for Amy Dineen. You have beds full of flowers all around your hotel."

"Yes, I do. Well, you go up to see Amy, the poor thing."

"I wonder if she is interested in the sailors."

"They seem to be interested in you, darling."

"Well, you know about sailors. It doesn't mean a thing."

The old man smiled. As clean and pink as a baby, dressed meticulously, he was as much a fixture of the hotel's handsome lobby as the bubbling fountain and the upward-curving grand stairway, as the gold-prismed chandelier. "Give Mrs. Dineen my best wishes, Nancy," he said gently.

"I will, Grampa. And I'll see you when I come down again."

"I'll be here."

He would be, too. She could not imagine the hotel without Eric's grandfather.

She found Amy half-sitting, half-reclining in her wheelchair out on the small balcony of her suite.

"Bad day," the nurse whispered to Nancy.

"I'm sorry. I won't stay." She went across the room and out.

"Amy," she said softly, "it's Nancy. I brought you some roses."

She held them close to the invalid's face.

"Can you smell them? They are pink and yellow. Very pretty."

Amy was weeping. She gestured the flowers away.

"I'll put them in water," Nancy said.

The nurse brought a bowl, and began to explain. "There's nothing really wrong," she said.

Nancy smiled at the woman, who was a new nurse. Service on Amy Dineen was a difficult duty. The nurses changed frequently. "Has Dr. Dineen been here?" she asked.

"Oh, yes. He is very good to his wife."

"He really is. I've known him, and Amy, for a long time. Besides, I work with Dr. Dineen in the hospital in the city."

"Oh?"

"I'm a surgical assistant. There! They are pretty, aren't they?"

"Very. I'll put them near the bed. She will want to go back there soon. I thought the music might interest her."

"It still might. I'll sit out there with her. If you'd like to take a break, I'm sure it would be all right."

"Yes, Miss —"

"Colburn. I'm Nancy."

"Are you related to . . . ?"

"Gayle? At the boutique? Yes, I'm her sister."

She went out to the balcony and sat down on a small chair beside Amy. She talked a little about the sailors and the bellhops' uniforms. Amy still wept. She dabbed at her eyes with a wad of Kleenex. Nancy brought some fresh sheets to her, then sat down again. She was sure Tim had been concerned about Amy's depression. Even for Nancy, this had seemed to increase lately.

For a half hour she sat quietly. Her visits often went this way. And often Amy did as she did that late afternoon. She fell asleep.

Amy could talk. She had, with difficulty, learned to talk. A little. She had learned to walk, too, a little. But for a couple of years, Nancy had not seen her walk.

When the nurse returned, Nancy rose and quietly went inside. "I'll be back tomorrow," she said softly.

"Thank you, Miss Colburn."

"It's Nancy. I'll be back." She slipped out into the hall.

She did come back, early the next morning, as early as seven-thirty, a short terry robe over her swim suit, bath clogs on her feet. "I wanted a swim before the water gets warm," she explained to the nurse. "How's Amy?"

"She's still in bed. I'm trying to get her to eat her breakfast."

"Maybe I can help. If you want a break . . ."

"Fifteen minutes maybe."

"Fine."

Again Nancy told Amy who she was. She talked about the sunrise, and the light on the water. "We have daylight saving time to thank for a pink and blue ocean," she said. "Don't you want your orange juice? It looks good. I'll hold the glass for you."

Amy drank some of the juice.

"Do you want your bacon cut, or do you like to eat it with your fingers? I do."

Amy's hand fell upon her wrist. "Do you know Tim?" she asked, her voice harsh.

Nancy put the knife and fork back on the tray. "Yes, I know him," she said.

"What is your name?"

"Nancy. You know me."

And tears again came into Amy's brown eyes. Drawing the blanket up to her chin, she lay back against the pillow and wept drearily.

Oh, dear, breathed Nancy. She guessed, if

she were blind, she might not want to hear about sunrise.

She waited.

"You're the girl," said Amy unexpectedly, and gasping a little, "who is trying to make out with my husband."

Now where had Amy got that phrase? It had been more than seven years since she had known and talked about such things. She'd been here in this hotel for that long, leaving the suite only for trips to the therapy rooms, or infrequently out for a wheelchair ride along the terrace in the winter sunshine. But — Oh, a maid could have gossiped with the nurse. Amy sometimes listened to the radio.

"No," said Nancy slowly, "my parents live near the hotel."

She could have said, "No, that's my sister."

She said nothing like that, but she did think about Gayle and Tim. At the time, she had thought it a shame that nothing could come of the attraction there was between them.

Tim was such a wonderful person. He could be a steadying influence on Gayle, about whom their parents worried.

Tim had also been wonderful to, and for, Nancy. He had suggested that she study nursing, getting a college degree. And then, again by suggestion more than advice, he had steered her into the surgical field.

Nancy loved the work, and knew that she was doing well. She was very grateful to Tim.

Should she try to explain all this to Amy?

But a glance showed her that Amy had fallen asleep. Nancy rose and met the nurse at the door. *"Shhhh!"* she whispered. "She drank some juice . . ."

And she slipped out.

Young Dr. Ritter had arisen that morning full of protests and irritations. He wished that this week could have been a routine of hard work but no interruptions in his thinking about what to do about the results of the Board examinations which he had taken. He knew the work, he should have made a good showing; he had needed only to freshen his knowledge on subjects that did not come up regularly in his hospital surgical service. He should have sailed right through the Boards. He had been confident — and now he should be able to make his plans.

But things kept coming up. Tim Dineen had chosen to come to the Beach at this particular time. He had driven over on Friday afternoon, planning to return after the staff meeting on Saturday.

Eric liked Tim, and respected him as a surgeon. He was glad when Dr. Dineen took on advisory work with the Beach Hospital's surgical service. Ordinarily he would have been glad or at least willing to have the week's staff meeting called for Saturday morning, though some of the other staff were not happy about it. A weekend was a weekend, except to resident doctors. Eric supposed the Chief had some particular problem to present to Dineen. As things turned out, he did not. At least, not while Eric was at the meeting. He had been called away at eight o'clock, or about then.

Another distraction had been the sailors. They had swarmed over the hotel, they had been on the beach . . . Two of them had to be hospitalized and had delayed the Chief Surgical Resident, keeping him from having dinner with Gayle. What substitute was a ham and cheese sandwich in a plastic bag and a lukewarm milk shake?

He grinned. Well, Gayle had been an acceptable substitute. She had been very sweet last night. Though disturbing, too. And not in her usual way of stirring his senses, firing his imagination, although

46

there was a little of that. He had wanted to make plans with Gayle about the things they would do now that the Board exams were out of the way. But Gayle, as always, was the one to decide what they would do, and even what they would talk about. So there had been the sandwich and the shakes, the damp sand. Not to mention the little two-somes of sailor and girl dotting the beach. And their talk had been about Tim Dineen.

Eric guessed a man like Dineen would seem romantic to women. His invalid wife, his profession — but Eric had never given any consideration to his appeal to young girls. He had heard Nancy say he was "great" to work with. That was professional.

But last night Gayle had brought out a side of Tim, without actually accusing him . . . Yes, she had, too! She had said she thought it was terrible for him to do what he had done with Nancy. She — Gayle — had "adored" him for a short time. But Gayle knew how to handle men. And she was old enough . . .

While Nancy was only fifteen when Tim had first brought his wife to the hotel. In a year or two she had let this — this Svengali direct her life. She said she liked what he had helped her do, but Gayle implied that the girl was still under Dineen's spell, and so had not done as most girls did — found some young men she could have fun with, and then one she could love and marry. Maybe Dineen was not aware of his influence. Maybe Eric Ritter should be the one to tell him, to break the news to the man. Yes, he would do that.

For the first part of the staff meeting, Dr. Ritter had watched Dineen, forming in his mind phrases of the things which he would say to him when the session broke up, if it ever did.

But there had come the telephone summons. Dr. Ritter had risen and gone out. The house telephone said only that he was needed at the hotel. His first thought was for his grandfather. Eighty years old. Then, there was his aunt who had had brain surgery two months ago. It just had to be a family matter!

He said he would go straight over, and would report as soon as he could. The operator could tell him nothing about the nature of the summons. She did say she would check him out of the hospital.

He would always remember walking swiftly along the wide, shining corridor of the hospital that morning. He could smell the breakfast trays being distributed. He replied to a half dozen "Good morning, Doc-

48

tor's." Maids, orderlies, a nurse who turned and looked after him — that sex appeal a doctor had for women. He went out the side door into the morning sunlight; he skirted and hopped over the hose of a man who was washing down the driveway. He crossed the street which bordered the hotel grounds, dead-ending at the beach. Gayle's home was on that road. And Nancy's, of course.

The sailors seemed to be gone. He didn't meet one. Though the lobby was busy. Being cleaned, mostly. Vacuums hummed; there was a canvas bag on wheels going along with a porter and his dustpan; ash trays were being emptied and wiped, a glass was retrieved from behind a couch cushion — newspapers, candy wrappers — a paperback book from under a chair, the breeze from the beach riffling its pages. Eric went to the desk.

"There was a call for me," he said, conscious of his white garments as being noticeable in the hotel lobby in the early morning. A few guests were about, coming and going from the coffee shop. He had passed a man and a woman out for a walk. There had been a few people on the beach.

"Oh, Eric!" It was the hotel manager coming down the stairs. "Will you come into my office?"

Eric felt his scalp prickle. "My grand-father . . . ?" he asked hoarsely.

"No, no. Come up here, just for a minute."

He could take anything else. He even looked at his watch. He wanted to get back before Dr. Dineen took off for the city.

Chapter 2

The hotel manager's name was Rich. Eric did not know him well. His uncle, Eugene Parmeley, had hired him when he — Parmeley — had agreed to come and supervise things. Eric's grandfather had lost his edge after "Gramma's" death last year. It seemed easier on the old man to turn responsibility over to a family member.

Dr. Ritter certainly could not take on the hotel. Frances was not well; she had needed surgery two months ago. So Parmeley came in and, according to Grampa, hired Rich to do his work.

All this settled into Eric's mind in the five seconds it took for him to go up to Rich's office on the mezzanine and to remain standing when Rich offered him a chair.

"I was sent for . . ." he jogged the man.

"Yes, I know, Dr. Ritter. We have had a — well — a misfortune here this morning, and it seemed better to call a family member . . ."

Eric frowned. "What sort of misfortune?" he asked sharply.

"Well, it seems . . . You know of course that we have a permanent guest on the fourth floor, an invalid, Mrs. Dineen?"

"Yes. Of course I know that! Has something happened to Amy?"

It could have. The woman was blind, and not able to care for herself.

"Yes, Doctor. Something has happened. The nurse called me and said she thought that Mrs. Dineen had died."

Eric turned sharply. *"Died?"* he cried.

"I'm afraid so. And maybe you realize that a death is always a crisis when it happens in a hotel."

"It's a crisis anywhere," said the doctor dryly. "Did you get the house doctor? And wouldn't the nurse *know* if the woman was dead?"

"I suppose she would, but she seemed to think that a doctor was needed. Of course we could have sent the — the patient — over to the hospital —"

"You're telling me that the house doctor wasn't around. And you want me to pronounce death, is that it?" Eric knew that he was sounding angry. Well, he was angry! He couldn't see any trace left of the uneventful weekend he had wanted.

"I'll go straight upstairs," he said stiffly.

"Yes, sir. If you like . . ."

"No, I won't need you. You stay down here and keep the matter quiet. Try not to upset my grandfather."

He did not hear Rich's reply. Swiftly he went down to the lobby and to the elevator. He must call Tim at once . . .

The elevator was down and open, but two men, joggers, followed him into it, and they made conversation with the doctor. The weather was perfect, they said, the sand great, and what did Eric think the fishing would be like.

"You can rent a boat down at the marina," he said as he left the elevator at the fourth floor. He was grateful that his training could be counted upon to keep his face and voice quiet.

The hotel was coming to life. Maids were in the halls; people were talking; TV's were turned on. Eric glanced at his watch. Eight-forty. He knocked on the door of Amy Dineen's suite, then opened the door and went inside. The room was in a clutter. An open newspaper on the floor, a small stack of folded sheets and towels in an armchair. The nurse came out of the bedroom, looking distraught, to say the least.

"I am Dr. Ritter," said Eric. "The house doctor seems to be missing."

"Yes, sir. Mrs. Dineen —"

"The manager told me." He brushed past the woman. She was probably thirty, and she didn't have her cap on. Her uniform was neat. He didn't know just why he thought she was on the verge of collapse. Her eyes perhaps, and the way she kept putting her fingers to her cheek.

The bedroom had been shaded against the morning sun. Eric had to go around the large wheelchair to approach the bed. "Open the blinds, please," said the doctor, taking out his stethoscope.

The patient — Amy — lay on the pillows; the head of the bed had been elevated and her head and shoulders had slipped to one side. One arm was still under the blanket and sheet, the other lay across her body, lax. Her mouth was slightly open. The doctor straightened her head and took out his pen light. "When did this happen?" he asked the nurse.

"I don't know . . ."

The doctor's head turned sharply. "You don't *know?*" he asked. He rolled back an eyelid.

"No, sir. She was sleeping. She did that way. She ate a little breakfast. I thought she might sleep, and I could bathe and dress her at any time. I took the tray out, and then I went for some linens. The maids clean the rooms, but I make the bed. So I went —"

"Did you leave her alone?"

"Only for a minute or two. She had had a visitor this morning. When I came back, she was sleeping. Then I sat down to wait. I began to read the paper."

Amy was certainly dead. The doctor folded the bedcovers back, and applied his stethoscope to the upper chest.

"When did you decide she had died?" he asked, his tone quiet.

"Oh — I came in to look at her, because she was sleeping so long — and she had tipped over the way she was. I couldn't find a pulse in her wrist —"

Of the hand that lay across her body.

The doctor lifted that hand and stripped the blanket down farther. He gasped.

The nurse did not.

He straightened and looked at her sharply. She was still stroking her cheek, but leaning against the paneled wall.

"You knew this had happened?" he asked sternly, gesturing to the blood-soaked mattress and the patient's bloody hand, her gown . . .

"Doctor, I was frightened. And the hotel — I thought —"

"Get me a wet cloth. Dampen a towel . . ."

He watched her closely. If she actually did collapse . . .

"When did you last see Mrs. Dineen alive and not hurt?" he asked, accepting the towel. He laid it on Amy's body, and rested the bloody hand on it. He wiped his fingers on the edge of the towel.

"I brought her medicine at seven o'clock," said the nurse, "and helped her to the commode. She was hard to handle. Then she got back to bed, I brushed her hair — and went for her breakfast tray."

"Yes." Eric looked about.

"She didn't eat much, and I set it out in the hall when she fell asleep. After I got the linens, you know."

And that tray already was down in the hotel's kitchens.

"Was there something sharp on the tray?"

"Oh, I don't think . . ."

"Just answer my question." He sounded like a detective or policeman. Both soon would be coming in.

"Well, there were dishes, but not broken. She had orange juice, a poached egg, toast, bacon. I guess there was a knife and fork. But maybe that girl . . ."

"What girl?"

"I told you she had a visitor. A young blonde girl. She said her sister worked in the boutique."

56

"Do you mean Nancy and Gayle Colburn? Was Nancy here early this morning?'

"Yes, sir. And yesterday evening, too. She brought flowers. Those roses. And this morning she came in again. Ready to go swimming from the way she was dressed. She said I could take a break. I got the linens, and Mrs. Dineen went to sleep, or I thought she did. Anyway, the girl left —"

"And you sat out in the other room while your patient bled to dcath from a wrist puncture. I'm just asking where she got anything sharp, Miss Gibson."

Her name plate said her name was Gibson.

"Oh, Doctor, I don't think a blind woman could have . . ."

"It looks as if a blind woman did! And a fork, or a table knife — Could she use her right hand at all? Do things for herself? Say, brush her teeth?"

"She could do a few things. Yes, sir. But —"

"I agree. This is bad. And we'll let the coroner decide the how's and when's."

He stood looking down at the dead woman, shaking his head. Things would have to be very carefully managed. "Has her husband been here?" he asked.

"Yes, sir. Yesterday afternoon, then he

came back for an hour or two. Stayed until bedtime."

"Did he come by this morning?"

"No, sir."

"Are you the only one who takes care of Mrs. Dineen?"

"Oh, no, sir. Another nurse, Mrs. O'Hare, relieves me. We take twenty-four-hour duty. Sleep on the couch."

Eric was surprised. He didn't know much about private duty nursing, of course. "When will your relief come in?" he asked.

"At noon. The work here isn't hard, Doctor. We arranged the hours ourselves. It seems — It seemed convenient."

"I see." Dineen, he was thinking, must be doing all right. A hotel suite, nurses around the clock . . .

"After I leave," he said, "you might call Mrs. O'Hare. He went into the sitting room and picked up the phone, asked to be connected with the hospital. "Just the board," he said.

Dr. Dineen had left for the city.

Eric again looked at his watch. Time was rushing by. He should be at the hospital . . .

"I'm going to speak to Mr. Parmeley," he told the nurse. "He'll know what to do. You're to stay here . . ."

"Not alone, Doctor!"

"Oh, don't be silly!" he cried, able at last to express some of his bottled-up protest. "You're a trained nurse. Stay here, don't touch anything. Not a thing! I'll be back in ten minutes or so. But don't let the maid in, and do not talk to her! Or anybody!"

It turned out to be a very long morning, and certainly not a quiet one. Of all the things Eric did, the least seemed to be to contact the Chief of Surgery, who told him to take the day off. "You sound as if you needed some recovery time."

Eric did need it. He should go to his room, or to the library, and perhaps check on the Board exam questions and their correct answers. He was beginning to wonder . . .

"Take a swim," suggested his roommate. "That relaxes me."

Eric nodded. "It does me, too," he agreed.

"And don't forget lunch," the other doctor called after him.

"I'm still behind on breakfast," said Eric. He had not talked about Amy to anyone since leaving the hotel, though he was sure the word was getting about. Tim should have come back . . .

He tried to remember the things he had been planning to say to Dineen. Way back to eight o'clock. After the staff meeting. They didn't seem important now, though he still could work up a little indignation . . .

What would Dineen do now? Stay on at the Medical Center in the city? He would very likely not continue his consultant service to the Beach Hospital. Or would he? If he still had an interest in one of the Colburn girls. Of course Gayle was preempted . . .

"I'll stop to see Gayle," he promised himself, even as he ran down the sandy slope and into the water.

It was relaxing, it did help get his thoughts into line. Several lines, but no longer tangled into a swirl. He would see Dineen, and maybe learn his plans. He would see Gayle. He would get some specific thinking done about his own affairs. He —

"Hi, Eric!"

Well, Nancy was a fish, really, and if this was her vacation, she would, naturally, be swimming a lot.

"Hi, Nancy," he said, rolling over. "You been here long?"

"Not really, this time. But I went in early this morning."

Before, or after, she had visited Amy?

He asked her.

"I heard about that," she said, her face sobering. "Are you ready to go in?"

"I think so." Shoulder to shoulder, they

struck for the shore.

"I had to pronounce her dead," said Eric when they reached the sand. He picked up a beach towel and hung it around his shoulders. He was a finely muscled young man. Brown as polished walnut.

Nancy was rubbing her hair with her own towel. Then she put on the terry robe. "Amy's been depressed lately," she said. "Do you think it was suicide?"

"There's to be a coroner's jury this afternoon. I have to be there."

"I hope Grampa fires that house doctor."

"Where was he?"

"Oh, I don't think he lives in the hotel. He has a house on the Beach road, about five miles."

"Is that good?"

"I don't know, Eric. My name isn't Ritter, so I don't know about running hotels."

He managed a smile. "Have you seen Dineen?" he asked. "Sit down for a minute, Nancy. Let your hair dry." He spread his beach towel, decorated with an enormous beer can.

She did sit down. "I haven't seen Tim," she said. "He was here last night."

"Yes. I was wondering what changes this might mean for him."

She nodded. Her chin was down on her

pulled-up knees, her hair thrown forward, concealing her face.

"How well do you know him, Nance?" he asked.

She turned her head to look at him. "I work with him. I've known him ever since he brought Amy here. That must be —"

"Seven years ago," said Eric. "How well do you like him? I don't mean as a doctor."

"Well, he *is* a doctor. But then, you're a doctor, too, and I don't think of you especially that way. Just what do you mean, Eric?"

"Gayle thinks you have had a crush on him."

"Ever since he first came here. Sure, I did. Gayle, too. All the girls did. But then, I've had a crush on you for about that long, too."

"Oh, Nancy!"

"Well, I have had. Not that anything comes of either crush." She guessed that Gayle had been talking to Eric. Maybe Tim had told her to straighten out things with the young doctor before she made definite plans to marry him. And Gayle's way was ever the indirect, the use of suggestion rather than stated facts. Before this her methods had irritated Nancy. She would, if necessary, have a talk with her sister.

She might even say a word or two to Dr.

Dineen. Not right away, of course. And she would be careful.

"Tim's been kind to me," she said to Eric after this long pause. "He helped me get into nursing school, he helped me specialize and work at the Center. But there was nothing *personal* in it, Eric."

"He likes you."

"Well, I should hope so!" She lay back on the sand and watched the noontime clouds piling up in the northern sky. They made castles and fortresses, and were shaded from dark gray to sparkling white. She stole a glance at Eric. He was staring at the ocean, which was creaming into little soft waves upon the sand, sliding back, to return . . .

"You're not worried about me, are you, Eric?" she asked.

"Not if you tell me you're all right. I think Gayle is concerned. You're young, and . . ."

Nancy scrambled to her feet, gathered up her towel and her beach bag. "Maybe Gayle is enough for you to worry about!" she said sharply. "I — well, good luck on your Boards. Won't the results be coming in soon?"

Eric groaned. "They will be," he said. "They will be. I hoped I could get a lot of time and peace of mind to get set for them and ready to decide finally what I shall do."

"And then this terrible thing has had to happen to Amy. I wonder why they called you."

"Instead of Dineen. Yes. I was called because the hotel was seeking to protect itself. They thought I could be counted on to be discreet."

"Were you?" asked Nancy.

He laughed shortly. "I didn't arrange for the body to be secretly buried," he said gruffly. "I think my uncle would have liked that."

"You talked to Grampa?"

"Eventually, yes. Everyone says he's failed, meaning in mental capacity. But he's still the smartest Ritter alive."

"I love him, too," said Nancy softly. "I'll be seeing you, Eric."

He nodded. "Yes," he said. "Yes, of course." He watched her go up the slope, stop to slip her feet into clogs, then cut across the hotel grounds toward her home. Nancy was a sweet girl, and pretty. He'd never realized how pretty she was. Gayle's beauty, he supposed, had always overshadowed the younger sister.

Nancy went home, kissed her mother to silence her usual protest at her walking "through town" in her bathing suit. The

Colburn house was not actually "in town" which extended inland from the beach, and Nancy could have pointed out many people on the street who wore less than she had on. She hung her robe in the hall closet, and kicked off her clogs. "I'll shower . . ." she said. "What's for lunch? I'm starved."

"Did you see Dr. Dineen?" asked her mother, following her.

"No. I'll try to see him this afternoon. But I did see Eric. I'll tell you about that at lunch."

On a Saturday, Andrew Colburn was at home for one o'clock lunch; he was a quiet man, well-respected by his family and the students of the girls' college at the far edge of Peter's Beach where he headed the English Department. Gayle had attended this school for a year. Nancy had not because of her decision to get a degree in nursing. Her father pretended to be affronted by this "slight" to his school.

Today, Veronica, his wife, a large, loving, outgoing woman, protested — as she always did — when he brought up the subject. Nancy and her father laughed at her.

After lunch, Nancy agreed to help her father weed the rose beds. "But I think I should try to find Tim and speak to him about Amy," she said.

"We should send flowers . . ." said her mother.

"Wait on that. I don't know what his plans will be. I'll go see him, and you can do something later."

"It's really a blessing, Nancy."

"Not if she killed herself, Mother. Tim's been good to her. He didn't expect her to live too long, but this —"

"Poor thing. I suppose she felt her life was useless."

Nancy, in denim cut-offs and white blouse, weeded the rose bed and talked to her dad. They were a lot alike — the slender, pretty girl, and the eyeglassed, quiet man. "You must be a great comfort to your students," she told him fondly when she went inside to "pretty up" and go down to the hotel.

Grampa Ritter would tell her where to find Tim.

"You look so pretty in a dress, dear," her mother said wistfully when Nancy came out wearing a thin dress flowered in shadowy patterns of pale green, soft rose, and blues. She had twisted her hair up away from her face into a soft roll at the back of her head. "The wind will blow your hair," her mother warned.

"I know. But this is as far as I am willing to go to make myself ladylike when I'm on vacation."

"Oh, my dear . . ."

"I'll wear gloves to church tomorrow," Nancy promised, going across the entry tiles toward the street. "Get Dad to come inside," she called back. "He's worked enough."

"I'll coax him. Give Tim our love."

"I'll do that," Nancy agreed.

The sailors were gone, but the hotel was busy, as it always was on a weekend. Nancy smiled and shook her head to see all the bright sweaters and strange hats that moved about the putting green. "Come to the beach and improve your golf game," she murmured to herself.

But there were a lot of people on the beach, too, and enough boats to be seen offshore to know that the marina was doing a good business.

She found Grampa in his usual chair in the lobby, and she waited patiently while various ones spoke to him. He'd seen her; he would make a time to let her talk to him. He did, too, holding out his hand to her. He introduced her to a man as "my pretty young friend."

Nancy smiled at him. And bent over, as

usual, to press her cheek to his. He held her hand. "Did you want something special, darling?" he asked.

"Yes. To find out where Tim might be."

"Oh, yes. Well, we've turned the Sea Bird Room over to him. It's down that hall, darling . . ."

"I know where it is, Grampa."

The Sea Bird Room was a small parlor off one of the main dining rooms. Brides used it for a dressing room, visiting dignitaries used it to receive friends, and, this afternoon, the many people who wanted to speak to Dr. Dineen in his bereavement were directed there.

It was a pretty room with good paintings of sea and birds, a gray-blue carpet, silvery brocade wall panels, a marble fireplace, mirrors and crystal wall sconces and a center chandelier. A damask sofa was set against the wall, silk-draped windows overlooked the beach, there were a few chairs.

And Tim. Flowers were in the room. Pink roses on a table before the mirror, vases of flowers on the mantel, a large arrangement of white gladiolas beside the couch.

Nancy recognized and spoke to several doctors who had come from the Center. The Administrator of the Beach Hospital was there, too. Several strangers.

"There's to be no funeral or visitation," she heard someone explain.

Nancy supposed the crowd was to be expected, though some of the people could only be curious. Tim must be tired, though he didn't show it too much. His face was customarily grave, controlled. He was wearing a dark gray suit, a white shirt and a plain, dark tie. His eyes lighted when he saw Nancy. He said something to the man who stood at his shoulder, and then he came across to her.

She held out her hand, but her eyes studied his face. "I shouldn't have bothered you," she said.

He looked back at the people who still stood or sat about. "Was there something special, Nancy?"

She flushed. "It can wait. At home, it seemed special. But . . . Of course, you know I am sorry. About Amy, I mean."

"You were the last to see her, weren't you?"

"I saw her this morning. She was crying."

He pressed his lips together. "Wait, will you?" he asked as he turned to speak to a woman in a white hat.

Nancy waited.

She spoke to a few people, then she sat on the couch, watched and listened. And after twenty minutes or so, only one couple remained. They left and Tim came across the blue carpet to her.

"Sit down," she said. "While you have a chance."

He did sit down. "I believe I am tired," he told her.

"Of course you are. You've had a bad day."

"I don't believe I really know what has happened," he said. "I'm numb."

"Could I get you some coffee? Or a drink?"

He touched her arm. "No. I want to talk to you. I heard that you had been to see Amy this morning."

"I did go. It's a habit I've formed whenever I'm at home. I don't know if she liked it or not."

"I liked it."

She smiled at him faintly. "This morning," she said slowly. "From what I've been told, she was dying when I was there. I should have known . . ."

"How would you? Her R.N. didn't."

Nancy stared straight ahead at the white gladiolas. "She even drank some orange juice. Amy did."

"Much?"

"No-o."

"You held the glass, I suppose."

"Yes. And of course there was a tube."

Tim sat forward on the couch cushion, his hands clasped between his knees. He stared at the floor.

"Then," Nancy continued, her voice quiet, "she seemed to drowse. At least, I *thought* she was falling asleep. She often did that way."

Tim said nothing.

After a minute or two, Nancy glanced at the door. Someone surely would come in. "What," she asked, "are you going to do?"

He straightened. "There's to be no funeral," he said.

"I didn't mean that. I meant *you*."

"I don't understand, Nancy. I'll continue to work, of course."

She had fully expected that. "Will you . . ." she asked, hesitated, then went on, "will you allow me to say something?"

"Of course." Now he was watching her face.

"Well, Amy's been sick for a long time . . ."

"Yes, she has. Ten years. That is a long time. We both were very young, ten years ago. Now —"

He was holding onto his control. As a doctor, he knew how to do that. Nancy had watched him in other difficult situations. She guessed that he had not, and would not, lose that control now.

"You see," he said, his tone that of a man explaining something. "In that ten years Amy changed. I did, too, of course, but not essentially. But she — she had become a different person. That happens to people who have strokes — brain damage of any sort. So — she became, not the girl I loved and married, Nancy. In the seven years you have known her, she has changed in appearance and nature."

Nancy nodded. Yes, Amy had changed.

"I came to pity her," Dr. Dineen was explaining, "but in the sense of desire and satisfaction, those things were gone. Gradually, yes, they were all gone. For Amy there no longer was hope, or a future. Now — we'll bury a shell, a precious box which once contained the girl I loved."

"I think Amy knew what had happened to her, Tim."

"Perhaps she did. Perhaps that was why —" He broke off. He took a handkerchief from his pocket and wiped the palms of his hands.

Nancy laid her fingers on his arm. "You've been wonderful, Tim," she said.

He put the handkerchief away. "No," he said. "I've been loyal and, at times, patient."

"You don't yet realize what has happened, do you?"

He said nothing.

"Now," said Nancy, her voice urgent. "Oh, do forgive me! But now you are free to go to Gayle and tell her you'll marry her. Now you are *free!*"

He frowned, his eyes were puzzled. "Is that . . . ?" he asked curiously. "Is that what you came here to say?"

Nancy stood up, and Tim did the same. He put his hands on her shoulders and looked down at her. Pale, shining hair, smoke-gray eyes . . . "I couldn't ever marry Gayle," he said gravely.

"But why not? I know you've been fond of her . . ."

"But I can't marry her, Nancy, dear. Because there are complications."

How could there be? "What complications?" she asked hardily.

"I am in love with Gayle's sister."

This shocked Nancy. She turned red, she turned white. He watched her. His hand still held her shoulder.

She shrugged free. "But you can't be!" she protested.

"I have been for some time."

"There's never been one thing between us. You've been like a kind, elder brother . . ."

"No, I have not."

"This is no time to tease me, Doctor!"

A man had come into the room, and she turned to leave.

"Wait, Nancy!" Tim called after her, but she left, hurrying after she reached the hotel corridor. Hurrying . . .

Chapter 3

"I'm in shock," she told herself. "Cold. Hot. Why did he say such a thing?"

Well, of course, Tim really *was* in shock. Later —

Nancy would forget what he had said to her. He would be grateful if she did. He did love Gayle. She remembered, way back when he first brought Amy to the hotel — she remembered coming upon the two of them embracing. Just last night he had been with her on the beach; they had talked earnestly.

"I'll just forget it," she said, starting for home.

She told her parents that she had seen Tim. "He's in shock," she told them. There was to be no funeral. Tim would continue to work . . .

"A man has to," said her father.

"I am going to change my dress," said Nancy. She felt — odd. As if she were tired. And sad. She had not shed a tear, yet she felt as if she had wept hard. A good swim might help, but it was after four o'clock — maybe she could go to the beach later — if she still felt this way.

She changed to a striped shirt and white shorts, white sneakers, and helped her mother get dinner ready. She agreed that it would be pleasant to eat out on the terrace. Would Gayle be home?

Her mother shrugged, and cut a tomato into wafer-thin slices. "When do you have to go back?" she asked her daughter.

"To the hospital? Wednesday. I had two weeks and a couple of sick leave days. I never get sick, so . . ."

Her mother had put the lamb chops on the broiler when the men came. They heard the door chime, they heard Dr. Colburn say, "What can I do for you, gentlemen?"

Mrs. Colburn looked at her chops. "I think I'll turn this off," she said.

Nancy murmured agreement. Her thoughts were back at the hotel. She hoped Tim would get some rest . . .

"Nancy!" It was her father calling. "Would you come in here, please?"

She glanced at her mother. What on earth . . . ?

"Take off your apron, dear," said Mrs. Colburn.

Nancy hung the apron over a chair back. "Who do you suppose . . . ?" she asked.

76

"Let's both go in and find out." Mrs. Colburn lifted the strap of her butcher's apron over her head. Her gray hair was always meticulously coiffed.

"I'm frightened," thought Nancy, smoothing her own hair. "I mustn't let Mother and Dad know . . ."

The Colburn living room was spacious, with a wide window that looked out at beach and ocean. There was a cathedral ceiling with dark beams, a stone fireplace and couches that flanked it, several woven reed chairs, shelves and shelves filled with books. A spacious, pleasant room that smelled always, though faintly, of wood smoke from the deep fireplace. This late afternoon it was fragrant, as well, from the copper bowl of roses on the coffee table.

This afternoon there were, as well, two men waiting with Dr. Colburn. He came to take Nancy by the hand. "This is my daughter Nancy," he said formally. "And my wife. Ladies, these men are here on police business. This one, in uniform, is Officer Bowens of the Beach police department."

Bowens was tall, slender, dark, and seemed embarrassed to be where he was. He ducked his head in acknowledgment.

The other stranger was an older man, a little pudgy. He was short.

"Mr. Eskridge is Assistant District Attorney," said Dr. Colburn, his voice crisp. His wife glanced at him.

"I am upset," her husband acknowledged the look. "These men say they want to question Nancy about Amy Dineen's death."

Nancy went to her father. "It's all right, Dad. I saw Amy this morning. Maybe I was the last one to talk to her. I think, even with a suicide, the authorities make an inquiry."

She saw the two men exchange glances. Her parents saw them.

"It has not been established, Miss Colburn," said Mr. Eskridge, "that the death was a suicide."

Nancy frowned. Eric had said — "Didn't the coroner say that?" she asked.

"No, ma'am, he didn't. He decided the cause of her death — but not who had inflicted the wound!"

"I see. But . . ." said Nancy, "I thought —"

"If you have first-hand knowledge, Miss Colburn . . ."

She didn't have. She had heard the radio announcement, she had heard talk. Eric had said . . . Hadn't he?

She shook her head. "When I saw her, she was alive," she said quietly.

"What time was that, Miss Colburn?" asked Mr. Eskridge. The policeman had

78

taken out a notebook, and he wrote something in it.

Dr. Colburn cleared his throat, and Nancy glanced at him. "If they are questioning you, Nancy," said her father, "you should have a lawyer."

"But, Dad . . ."

"How old are you, Miss Colburn?" asked the District Attorney.

"I am almost twenty-three, but —" she smiled at her father. "I listen to my father."

"Good!" said Mr. Eskridge.

"Are you making any charge against Nancy?" asked Mrs. Colburn.

"We would just like her to come downtown with us and answer a few questions."

"And of course she will do that," said Dr. Colburn. "With a lawyer present. I'll bring her to your office tomorrow, sir."

"No, sir. Tomorrow is Sunday, and we think we should talk to her tonight. You may drive her down, if you like."

"I'll do that." He showed the two men out, came back, and picked up the telephone. "You might want to put on a dress, Nancy," he suggested.

Feeling as if she were encased in a plastic container of some kind, transparent, but confining, Nancy did change. She put on a skirt instead of the white shorts, brown slippers instead of the sneakers, she tied a scarf around her hair. She reassured her mother as best she could. "Dad's getting the College's attorney, Mother. And I don't mind answering their questions."

She said the same thing when they were issued into an office at the courthouse. Mr. Eskridge was there, and a stenographer. Mr. Heser said that he would represent Miss Colburn. He hoped that her father could be present?

"Yes, of course. Sit down, Professor."

The office was a nondescript room. There was a square desk behind which Mr. Eskridge sat; behind him was the stenographer with his little machine. There were several chairs, wooden, with arms. A window that looked out upon a brick wall; Venetian blinds were tilted to the half-open position. Nancy shivered.

"I don't see any reason why I should not answer their questions," she said to Mr. Heser, who had just told her not to unless he agreed. "I didn't *do* anything to Amy! And if her death was not a suicide, I want to help find out who caused it. I —"

"Nancy," said her father. "Do what Mr. Heser says."

"But if they are going to question me, or hold me, because I was *there*, why, plenty of others were there, too. Miss Gibson, the nurse, and the room maid — even Tim. What motive do they think I would have — ?" Her panic was rising rapidly.

"Let us just ask our questions, Miss Colburn," said Mr. Eskridge.

"And I'll say which ones you should answer," said Heser. "Though I would like a chance to talk to you first, in private." He looked expectantly at the District Attorney.

"Later, if necessary," said that gentleman. "This is all preliminary."

"All right, if you'll remember that it is."

"We had a little difficulty locating Miss Colburn this afternoon," said the District Attorney.

"Why, I was at the hotel," said Nancy, in surprise. "I went to see Dr. Dineen and offer my sympathy to him. He doesn't think I killed Amy!"

"Nancy . . ." said Mr. Heser gently.

"Well, they are holding me for her death, aren't they?"

He rose and came to her side. "I expect they have questioned other people, my dear. Even Dr. Dineen."

This did shock her. "As good as that man has been to Amy? How could they think . . . ?"

"If you would quiet down, my dear, we

81

could get through this more quickly."

He turned to Mr. Eskridge. "Perhaps if I would question her? If you would indicate to me the line you want to follow . . ."

"It is irregular, Mr. Heser."

"It is. But we might get to your objective more quickly."

"I'll get to it, sir, even if I have to file charges."

Nancy gazed at him, her face white. "I'm sorry," she said meekly. "It's just — well, I feel I shouldn't be here."

"All right, then. Let Mr. Heser and me ask our questions."

She sat quietly then, looking down at her hands. Her father sat beside her. He was most distressed.

"You understand, don't you, Professor," said Mr. Eskridge, "that our only way of deciding if there has been foul play, if someone cut Mrs. Dineen's wrist so that she bled to death, is to question everyone who might have done such a thing? Up to this point we are making no charges. We are just trying to find out what happened."

"I understand," said Dr. Colburn. "Do you, Nancy?"

She nodded, but said nothing.

"All right then. Nancy, did you know Mrs. Dineen well?"

She drew a deep breath, and glanced at Mr. Heser. He nodded.

"I don't think anyone knew her *well*, sir. She was terribly handicapped. She had had an accident that caused brain damage. She was blind, and was restricted in her ability to walk and talk. But I went to see her, and tried to talk to her. I took her flowers — things like that. I have been doing that for a long time. Almost ever since her husband brought her to the hotel."

"Meaning to be kind?"

"Well, yes, I suppose so. I was sorry for her. She didn't have many others to do things of the sort."

"She had nursing care, however."

"Oh, yes. Around the clock. A nurse was with her all the time."

"*All* the time, Miss Colburn?"

"Well, the nurse might be in another room, or leave for a few minutes on some errand."

"You are a nurse yourself, aren't you?"

"Yes, sir. I have been one for almost three years. But I don't do bedside nursing. I work in the operating rooms. I am called a surgical assistant."

"And you know Dr. Dineen?"

"Of course. Yes."

"Does he like you?"

"*I'm in love with Gayle's sister,*" *Tim had said.*

Nancy frowned. "I've always thought that he liked me. But —"

"Just answer the question, Nancy," said Mr. Heser.

"I did answer it, the best I could. How does anyone know if, really, she is liked?"

"Did Mrs. Dineen ever indicate whether she liked you or not?"

"Oh, for heaven's sake, Mr. Eskridge! Amy — Amy — A person like that — they take likes and dislikes. They are not rational. If you've ever known anyone who has had a stroke! Amy never showed active dislike toward me, if that's what you mean!"

"Has anyone suggested that she did not like Nancy?" asked Nancy's father.

"I'm afraid that I must ask the questions, Professor."

"And you've asked them, from Tim, and the woman's nurse . . . *Did she* tell you that Amy did not like Nancy?"

Mr. Eskridge shuffled his papers.

"Just what were your relations with Dr. Dineen, Miss Colburn?" he asked coldly.

Gibson, the nurse, had said to this — this *bloodhound!* — that Amy did not like Nancy.

"I don't understand," said Nancy just as coldly.

"You were friends?"

"I think so."

"Are you living here in Peter's Beach?"

"You know I am not. I live and work in the city."

"You work with Dr. Dineen, perhaps?"

"I work in the hospital operating rooms. Dr. Dineen is a surgeon. Yes, sometimes I work with him."

"And I don't advise you to ask, or Nancy to answer, your next question, Eskridge," said Mr. Heser firmly.

Nancy looked at him. "I live in one of the apartments which the hospital makes available to its nurses," she said sweetly.

"Whatever anyone has told you," added her father.

Mr. Eskridge laid down one paper, picked up another. "Miss Colburn," he said, "Perhaps you know that Mrs. Dineen died from the loss of blood because of a puncture wound in her left wrist."

"It was told on the radio. So everyone must know that."

"I suppose so. Now! We have had two people tell us that Mrs. Dineen had not the ability to self-inflict such a wound. How do you feel about that?"

Nancy tipped her head back in a gesture of thought, consideration. "I think she could have . . ." she said. "Given a weapon. Scissors or something of the sort."

"She was not paralyzed?"

"Not really. She had had therapy. She could use one of her hands pretty well. It was — let's see — yes, her right hand. She fed herself when she wanted to. She could walk a little, with help. And talk when she wanted to."

"I see. But she was gravely handicapped?"

"Oh, yes. She certainly was."

"Do you think she might have recovered to any degree?"

"I don't know, Mr. Eskridge. I am not a doctor."

"And I've heard nurses make that kind of reply before."

"Yes, sir. It's trained into us."

"Yes. Now! You said, I think, that you lived in the city. How long has it been since you have lived at home here on the Beach?"

"Oh — let's see . . ."

"Five years," said her father.

Nancy smiled at him. "That's right," she agreed. "Three years in school, two registered and working."

"How do you happen to be here now?"

"I am on vacation."

"Did you drive down? Do you have your own car?"

86

"I drove down with Dr. Dineen. I don't have a car, but I could have used the bus."

"I see. And, you say, you always go to see Mrs. Dineen."

"I usually do, yes."

"In the two weeks you've been at home —"

"It has been two weeks, but how did you know . . . ?"

Mr. Heser touched her arm, and he shook his head at her.

Mr. Eskridge nodded. "Don't make the Prosecutor angry," he said, smiling. "That's good advice. And to answer *your* question, Miss Colburn, someone did tell me that. Your sister, I believe. I told you that I had been looking for you."

"Yes, sir."

"How often in that two weeks did you go to see Mrs. Dineen?"

"Well, not every day. But I often did."

"In the early morning?"

"At various times. Evenings — but I have gone two or three times in the morning. When I'd come to the hotel to swim. Grampa — Mr. Ritter — lets me use their beach."

"I see. I mentioned your sister. Does she swim with you?"

"Not early in the morning."

"All right. Does she — did she go to see your friend, Amy Dineen?"

"When I went? No, she didn't."

"Did she go at all?"

"You should have asked her."

"I may have done that. I talked to her — when I was hunting you —"

Nancy waited.

"Your sister said she didn't think Mrs. Dineen would have been able to self-inflict the wound in her wrist. Did you tell her that?"

"No, I couldn't have." And Eric or Tim would not have said that either, but perhaps Miss Gibson, or the other nurse, might have said such a thing to Gayle. Either doctor would have blasted a nurse who talked so to outsiders. But Amy frequently was the subject of talk throughout the hotel among its employees.

"Miss Colburn!" said Mr. Eskridge, to regain her attention. She glanced at him.

"Yes, sir?" she said. Politely.

"Were you alone with Mrs. Dineen when you visited her yesterday or this morning?"

"The nurse was in and out."

"Did you tell her to leave?"

Gibson had told him that. Gibson was a witch! Nancy looked at Mr. Heser. "I may have . . ." she said quietly. "That is often done when there is a chance for another nurse to give the duty nurse a break."

"I see. What was Mrs. Dineen's manner last night and this morning?"

"Why — about as usual."

"Did she talk?"

"A little. She asked me if I knew her husband."

"But didn't she know . . . ?"

"She was a sick woman, Mr. Eskridge. Her brain had been injured. Those people are lucid sometimes, sometimes not. We don't consider either condition too significant. They weep readily, they —"

Mr. Eskridge wrote something on the paper before him. "Did she weep this morning?"

"Yes. And then, immediately afterward, she fell asleep."

"Could it have been a faint?"

Nancy shrugged. "It could have been. I thought she was asleep. I told the nurse that she was."

"When you left?"

"Yes."

Someone came to the door with a message for Mr. Eskridge. He excused himself and departed. Nancy and her father and the attorney waited uncomfortably.

"Does he really think I killed Amy?"

Nancy asked Mr. Heser.

"I don't know, Nancy. These fellows question everybody remotely connected with a crime." He glanced at the stenographer who maintained his air of disinterested attention. "And they always act as if the person being questioned is the guilty one. Eskridge — It's hard to figure what he is thinking."

Nancy wished the stenographer had left with Eskridge. She had a dozen questions to ask Mr. Heser.

Eskridge was gone for only three minutes, and again he apologized when he returned. "I think we can wind this up quickly," he said, looking at his watch.

"It's a rather irregular sort of meeting anyway, isn't it?" Mr. Heser asked him.

"You're right, it is. I like to keep these things informal. Besides, in this case, a big item with me is consideration for the Ritter family and for Professor Colburn. There's Dr. Dineen, as well."

"And justice?" asked Mr. Heser suavely.

"I'll see that that is considered, in time, sir."

"I hope you will, Mark. I sincerely hope you will."

The District Attorney rummaged among the papers and objects on the desktop and came up with a long, silvery object which he held by the point and swung up and down. "You know what this is, Nancy?" he asked, closely watching her face.

She brushed a lock of hair away from her cheek. "Of course I know. It's a nail file."

"Would it be yours?"

She reached her hand to take the file. "I don't think so," she said. "Are my fingerprints on it?"

"Nancy!" her father breathed.

Mr. Eskridge smiled. "Nobody's fingerprints were on it," he said. "Do you have such a file?"

"Similar to it, yes."

"Where do you keep it?"

"Oh, I keep one in my travel kit. And I have one in a drawer in my room at the hospital."

"In your purse?"

"No, I keep an emery board there. But lots of women do carry files. I don't have pretty nails, you know. Long ones slit the rubber gloves we wear." She spread her small hands; the fingers looked childlike, the pink nails squared off neatly. "Where did you find that one?" she asked.

"I might as well tell you. When the hospital bed was returned to the rental agency from which it had been secured, a file was found in the thick pile of the carpet a little way under the bed, and about three feet down from the head of it."

"On the right or left side?" asked Nancy quietly.

"Don't you know?" Mr. Eskridge countered.

Mr. Heser stood up. He put his hand on Nancy's shoulder. She looked up at him in protest.

"Why shouldn't I answer him?" she cried. "For that matter, why should he sit there questioning me? If he is going to believe one answer I make, why shouldn't he believe me when I say I did not hurt Amy?"

She leaned back in her chair, visibly trying to control herself. She thought of familiar, good things, the operating room, and its clean, understandable chaos, busy, noisy, bright, sometimes hot. The green garments of the doctors and nurses, the flash of chrome, and the doctors' instruments. Tim's voice . . .

Could he — Did he think — that she could have hurt Amy?

No. Of course not.

She thought of the wide, clean walks between the hospital buildings, the sunlight and shade, the people — doctors striding along, their white coats unbuttoned, pretty nurses chattering, laughing, calling out to her. "Hi, Nancy! How's the girl?"

She thought of the beach here at home, with the ocean water green and sparkling into little choppy waves, rimmed with diamonds in the sunlight.

She gulped.

Mr. Eskridge was rearranging his papers. "Did I ask if you were alone with Mrs. Dineen this morning?" he asked, then answered himself. "Yes, I have that."

"I imagine the nurse told you," said Nancy. "Did she tell you the exact time I was there? And just when she found out that her patient was dead? Because Amy definitely was not dead when I was there!"

"No one suggests that she was, Miss Colburn."

"Miss Gibson would not want to be blamed."

The papers rustled against each other.

"But you suspect *me* of being responsible!" Nancy cried. "You've decided that I cut Amy's wrist and left her to die."

Her father rose and bent over her. "Nancy, you must stop this!" he said firmly.

"But, Dad —"

"I know. I know. I too am shocked at any such suggestion."

"Dr. Colburn," said Mr. Eskridge.

"Nancy. I have made no decision on anyone's guilt. As your sister said to me, I *hope* you did not do it!"

"Gayle said *that?*" asked Nancy, her face white.

"She was distressed at the suggestion that you could have done it. Frankly, I myself am distressed. But I am afraid that I must recommend that you be held for questioning by the grand jury. To determine whether you should be charged and held for trial."

"I can't see that you have any grounds for your decision," said Mr. Heser angrily.

"I think you do, sir. Miss Colburn had the opportunity; she had the means . . ."

"And the motive?"

"That is to be established. Just now, I think we must hold her."

"In jail?" asked Nancy, her voice rising in panic.

"Don't worry," said Mr. Heser. "We'll have you out again . . ."

"This court does not readily grant bail, Heser, in a case of homicide or premeditated murder."

Nancy stared at him. Her father did; he was shaking.

"I'll send a matron," said Mr. Eskridge, glancing at the stenographer, then briskly leaving the room, all of his papers and notes, even the slender, gleaming nail file, zipped into a blue plastic envelope.

Nancy sat down on the chair. "What do we do now?" she asked.

"We'll get busy," Mr. Heser promised.

Nancy looked up at him. She reached for her father's hand and held it. "How?" she asked. "How does a person prove he doesn't do a thing? That he hasn't done it?"

"Well, he — you can establish an alibi. Or, of course, produce the person who did commit the deed."

"I don't even know how long it would take a person like Amy to bleed to death. So what sort of alibi . . . ? Besides, I am sure this was suicide."

"Could it have been, Nancy?"

"Of course. She was depressed. Her mental condition — She could have had the file hidden for days. Could they prove whose it was? When she might have got it? The nurses know she could use her right hand. The therapists know it. Of course it was suicide! Can't they prove that?"

"I don't know, Nancy. If she had made other attempts . . ."

"And he talked about motive. What motive could I have had?"

"Well, if anyone thinks you were — are — in love with Dr. Dineen . . ."

She flushed. "I am not. He's Gayle's — has been since he first came here."

Her father touched her hand. "You are forgetting Eric, darling. Gayle is not in love with Tim."

"Gayle is not in love with anyone except Gayle!" Nancy cried, then she dropped her face to his shoulder. "I'm sorry, Dad. I shouldn't have said that." She kissed him. "I'm sorry that I did this thing to you and Mother. Tell her . . ."

"What shall I tell her, my dear? What did you do? I am sure it was nothing that you should not have done."

"But I —"

"Know the truth, my dear. Hold it fast. I shall. Meanwhile, be brave. This soon will be over." He kissed her warmly.

"You look so tired," said Nancy sadly.

"But not afraid." He smiled at her, and she nodded.

"I'll try . . ." she promised.

The matron had entered the room. Mr. Colburn said he would go home. Mr. Heser promised to "stick around."

Nancy, afterward, remembered the events that followed in brief pictures that flipped over without being really seen. The police matron's blue blouse and skirt, her badge. A hall. Steps down, cement steps. And down again. A bright room. Fingerprints made. Her fingers wiped with a damp cloth. People talking . . .

Did Tim know what was happening to her? If he did, wouldn't he come and make some sort of row? He was good at rows.

Or — did he, maybe, think she had killed Amy? That she did it to free him for Gayle? She remembered that she had gone to him in the Sea Bird Room and urged him to marry Gayle now. The Sea Bird Room. Blue carpet, pink roses — and Tim looking tired . . .

They took off her clothes — she must shower, they said — and dress again. Canvas shoes, too big for her slender feet.

"Why can't I have my own clothes?"

"We'll take care of them."

Then there were bars. A cell. Stone-floored, one grated window, high up. A cot, a shelf, a stool, a basin and a toilet. A blanket folded on the foot of the cot. A man brought food. "Supper," he called it.

They had taken her watch, but the light said it was getting late. She was not hungry. She thought of the lamb chops at home. Had her father driven carefully? What was he telling her mother?

There were other people nearby. She

could hear them talking and making sounds. Feet scraped, metal objects clashed together. A bell rang. Women talked. Men, too.

". . . dame killed out at the hotel. Got a suspect who'd been in her room — victim was an invalid. Suspect went to see her early in the mornin' —"

Nancy lay down on the cot. The suspect. Early in the morning she had gone to see Amy, the victim. She had gone to see Tim, too, later in the day. After she had seen and talked to Eric. *He* had not appeared to think Nancy was a suspect. Just what had he said? That he had pronounced death, and thought that Amy had killed herself. He probably wrote that on the certificate. Evidently that was not enough. But, anyway, he thought Amy was capable . . .

Nancy sat straight up. She must remember that! If Eric thought . . . He would *know!*

She went to the door of the cell. "Could I have a paper and pencil?" she called. Twice.

"No," someone finally answered. "Not tonight."

Well . . .

After talking to Eric, she had been at home for a time, then she had dressed in her flowered voile and had gone to see Tim. To beg him . . .

He'd said he was in love with Gayle's sister. Which, maybe, was the craziest thing said on the long, crazy day.

She lay down again and turned her face away from the unshaded light bulb which had been switched on. She guessed "suspects," or inmates, or whatever, didn't get to turn their own lights on and off.

A man, a guard, she supposed, came for her tray and protested that she had not eaten anything. "It ain't bad," he told Nancy.

"I wasn't hungry." She went back to the cot.

She heard — Maybe she thought she heard, maybe she dreamed . . .

At first, she knew there was talk, voices, farther down the hall. Talk between other prisoners, between the guards — she didn't know, and at first she did not listen.

Then — the words began to take on meaning.

She heard her own name — her father's —

"She don't look like she'd kill anyone."

"Maybe she didn't."

"Well, I know a fella works at the hotel — seems her sister works there, too . . ."

Gayle. Who managed the boutique, a glittery place of expensive clothes, beach robes, swim suits, tennis dresses — bright jewelry, exotic perfumes . . .

"*She* says our girl probably did do it . . ."

The Assistant District Attorney had said the same thing. The "D.A." — heretofore considered only by Nancy as a feature of some TV program.

"Oh, she was *sorry!* She said she certainly hoped her sister had not . . ." That would be Gayle!

There was a break in the conversation. Some activity down the hall — Then it resumed. Now Nancy was listening alertly.

"There sure was a man. If our girl had interest in the woman's husband — a doctor, I think. Not old. Maybe he was behind her doin' it. If she had a thing for this guy, she'd want him free . . ."

"What did *he* want?" This caused laughter, of a sort. Nancy shivered.

"*Couldn't* divorce her," said a louder voice. "Seems his wife was afflicted some way."

Nancy put her hands over her ears. She didn't want to hear more. Because right there, spelled out, was the D.A.'s motive. A case could be made.

Tim had coaxed or — in some way — he had got Nancy to kill his "afflicted" wife. And he —

Wouldn't he tell them — tell somebody — that he was in love with Gayle? He had not meant what he'd said yesterday — No. It was today! Only this afternoon! When he had said . . .

Nancy sat up, she got to her feet, she took the cup hung beside the basin and drank some water. She walked about and wished that the light could be turned off. She wanted to think.

She stood on the stool and looked out through the bars of the small window. She could see the corner of the building — a street light — the window was closed.

If only she could hear the ocean! The sound of it might help clear her mind so that she could think. But she could not hear a thing except the voices and noises down the hall. The jail was downtown in Peter's Beach. She knew that the beach itself and the surf was a good mile away. She had known where the town jail was without ever giving it actual attention. She . . .

The jail? The — *jail?*

She, Nancy Colburn, was actually in JAIL?

She whirled about, she looked at the ceiling, at the floor, the walls — at the bars of the door between her and the hall. Between her and freedom. She went across to those bars, and ran her hands down two of them. Her hands, small, strong — clean — were her hands. And the bars —

But she was Nancy Colburn! A well-behaved girl. A young lady, as her mother had trained her to be. She wore a hat to church, and white gloves. The District Attorney knew that she was a nice girl, he'd said something like that to her father. The jailer, or whoever, who had picked up her supper tray, had said that she would eat alone . . .

"Because you think I'm a murderer?" she had asked him bitterly.

"No, ma'am. Because you're a nice young girl. We don't get many of your sort."

But they had "got" Nancy. They seemed to have a right to get her. And keep her? For how long? What would happen next? She had heard someone say she was being held for the investigation of murder. Mr. Eskridge had mentioned a grand jury. Would there be a judge? Not bail — she'd heard that there would not be. But wouldn't there be some way to protest? What was it called? Yes. Appeal. Oh, she wished she knew more about these things! Just because she had not thought she would ever need to know . . .

Someone down the hall called, "Lights!" A woman with a voice as loud as a man's.

Nancy went over to the cot. She hoped she would be tired and drained enough to sleep.

To sleep in jail. And suddenly she felt tears hot in her eyes, tears were running down her cheeks. Well, why not?

She was angry, she was afraid — What was she going to *do?* Oh, someone would prove that she had not killed poor Amy. "The truth comes out." She believed that. But maybe it would, and maybe it wouldn't. If she spent time in prison, or even if she were just accused, then acquitted — What hospital would ever let her work?

No. On this bright afternoon, everything had ended for Nancy Colburn, almost twenty-three.

The day had begun all right. She had gone to see Amy, she had swum — Twice that morning, she had swum. The second time she had met Eric and they had sat on the beach.

Even now she could see his brown shoulder beaded with drops, and she had watched sea brine dry on his cheek.

Dear Eric. He would not think she could have — Eric had pronounced death. A suicide.

The lights went out. There was a glow in the corridor. Nancy lay on the cot, still thinking.

★ ★ ★

She thought about her mother and father, and what they must be saying to each other, and feeling. They would question Gayle.

And what would Gayle say or do? She was entirely unpredictable. Except that Nancy knew her pretty well, not always liking what she knew. If Gayle guessed what Tim had said about loving Gayle's sister, she might say or do a dozen things. *She* was in love with Tim, and had been for years. When he first brought Amy to the hotel . . .

Gayle was beautiful. Gayle laughed, and danced — She must have seemed like a drink of ice water to a thirsty man. Tim had given her a rush. Nancy, at fifteen, had seen them together, and had had her young emotions churned into turmoil.

But — after a time — Tim had drawn back. Nancy could only guess why. Getting to know him, growing up to be closer to his own age, knowing him at work, she had decided that wisdom and discretion might have taken over.

But Gayle thought he still loved her, she thought he did now. And if she meant to win him — she might even give Eskridge and his friends a motive for what they claimed Nancy had done. She could say that, yes, her little sister had a passion for the doctor who had been so helpful to her.

Nancy stared at the ceiling and imagined the scene. Her parents would have summoned Gayle. Perhaps she came of her own accord when she heard about Nancy's arrest . . .

Nancy gulped over the word.

At home — They would sit in the living room, or perhaps out on the patio. Her mother would sit beside her father. Each still wore the clothes they had worn an hour or two before, or three . . . Her mother in a lavender striped dress, her father in his neat blue jacket and gray slacks. Gayle could be dressed in almost any way. Casually, or very carefully, but always smartly. She loved bright colors and wore them well. Her dark hair, her vivid, lovely face — she wore jewelry often. Usually. Perhaps tonight she would have on that citron-colored linen, and several gold chains. Earrings, of course.

She would have come to the house, kissed her mother, whom she called *Mums,* and hugged her father. Gayle was a tall girl, and demonstrative.

She would say all the expected things, that this was terrible. Who would have thought their little Nancy . . . ?

"But she didn't do it, Gayle!" Mrs. Colburn would protest.

And Gayle would smile patiently.

"But, Mums . . . We have to face the fact that maybe she did. In fact, I am beginning to be just dreadfully afraid that she came home especially to do this. She did want Tim to be free."

"Well," Dad would say, "any number of people hoped he might be."

"Yes, we did!" Gayle would agree, curling her long legs under her in the big chair. "But Nancy — she loves that man —"

"She's grateful to him for his help. That's why she did so much for Amy."

"Gratitude is one thing, Gayle . . ." her dad would point out.

"And love another. Yes, it is different. My theory is that Nancy got beyond her depths. She could be grateful to Tim, but when that feeling turned to love and desire . . . Oh, it is all so distressing! I wish we could have been warned, and might have prepared Nancy —"

"Good heavens!" Nancy now said below her breath. Did Gayle weep? Oh, yes. She very likely did.

And her parents would protest and assure Gayle that she could not really think —

"It isn't what I want to think, dears. But look at the facts. Amy was in a deplorable condition. She could not get well. And poor

Tim . . . This was certainly in Nancy's mind, a matter for mercy killing. She knew what to do, and she had the opportunity to do it. She was allowed to come in and out of Amy's room. The nurses allowed her to sit beside Amy's bed. Nancy knew, from her training, how to cut Amy's wrist, and leave the helpless girl to bleed to death. A mercy killing. Merciful, but illegal."

On her cot, Nancy shivered. It all sounded so logical, so possible. Except that —

Her mother and father would continue their protests to Gayle. Nancy could not have done such a thing!

"Oh, yes, she could," Gayle would repeat. "It makes me *sick* to think that she did do it. But she *could!* She was — she is crazy about Tim — and she knew *how* to help him!"

Perhaps her father mentioned the nail file. Gayle had talked about Nancy's training — Wouldn't she have used a better, sharper instrument?

"Not one she'd brought from the hospital, Dad. She wasn't freeing Tim just to shut herself up in prison. But a nail file . . . Anybody — any woman would have one."

"Oh, Gayle." Because Nancy had said exactly the same thing. Her father would have remembered that, and been frightened.

And of course Gayle would comfort him. Them. "We have to face this awful thing," she'd tell them. "And try to help her in any way we can."

But her parents would still protest. Nancy was Gayle's sister, they would point out. "You should love her . . ."

"I *do* love her!" Gayle would insist. "But not blindly, darlings. I'm sorry that I can't just say that Nancy didn't do it, and believe it."

"And she could not. Say it, or believe it. She really could not."

Her mother might say that she simply would not have such a situation in their family. But the poor thing did have it.

Now Nancy turned on the cot, and turned again. She sat up, she walked about. And — she faced herself in that stark, dimly lighted jail cell.

Here she was, all upset over a conversation which she had imagined, manufacturing it out of nothing. Gayle had not said any of those things. She wouldn't say them. Why should Nancy even think she could?

She and Gayle were not too far apart in ages. Three years, almost. But it was enough that, from birth, they had had almost nothing in common. They didn't look alike. Nancy had played with dolls; Gayle rode her bicycle, skated, and played baseball. Nancy went to dancing school; the boys taught Gayle to dance. Boys liked Nancy — one boy at a time. Boys swarmed about her sister. But there had never been real conflict between the two girls. The only hurt Gayle had ever done her sister was to take Eric and plan to marry him.

It would be better —

Nancy stopped short in her pacing of the cell. For five minutes she stood staring before her.

Was that why she had wanted Tim to marry Gayle, now that he was free, and had told him . . . ?

Could such a thing be?

She should have let things alone! But she had *told* Tim — Oh, she should not have done that!

Shivering, Nancy lay down on the cot and drew the rough blanket up to her chin. She hoped its warmth would help her sleep. She didn't want to think any more.

But she did think. Again and again she went over the session with Mr. Eskridge. *He* had quoted Gayle. She *hoped* her sister had not done it. The men down the corridor had quoted her. Hadn't they? She couldn't remember . . . Everything was so blurred.

Why would Gayle say anything? She

didn't *know*. But she was a talker, and if people were talking around her, she would certainly join in and say something. And be quoted.

But *why?* Even if she thought Nancy had killed Amy. Mercifully or not. Why would she speak out? Did she know more than Nancy did? Or the police? Or her parents?

Did she think that Tim, perhaps —

Oh, good heavens, no!

But who did do it? Who?

Amy herself? Eric had thought she had. If Amy could manage a knife, or scissors — or a nail file . . .

Chapter 4

Dr. Ritter — who had been excused from duty for twelve hours after his being called to the hotel because of Mrs. Dineen's death, and then needing to talk to the hotel people, to the police, to testify at the coroner's inquiry, with only a brief free hour when he had gone for a swim and had talked to Nancy — at six o'clock that same evening went on thirty-six-hour duty at the hospital.

This was only fair. The resident on duty the night before had taken an extra twelve hours to relieve Ritter. Now Ritter must make up the time. Perhaps they would not be busy, though he didn't really expect that. Not with the way this week seemed to be going.

Thinking of these things, the doctor stood at the window of the surgical suite corridor and looked down at the parking lot, and without at first really seeing it, at the activity of the trash disposal crew. This was a big item, he realized, to dispose of all the waste from a two-hundred-bed hospital — the paper, the dressings, the food tray liners, dead flowers, bottles and used syringes . . .

Stalwart men were wheeling what appeared to be heavy carts out from a wide door below his window. These carts were piled high with plastic bags — yellow, red, green, black — according to the sort of refuse they contained. They were pushing their carts, or dollies, across the blacktop to a large square edifice built of cinder blocks. The carts were pushed up a ramp, where the bags were lifted by hand and deposited into an open maw. Even with thermal glass protecting him, Eric could hear the shouts of the men and the grinding of the compactors.

There did seem to be an awesome lot of detail attached to running a hospital. He sighed.

But his weekend of concern about the results of his Board exams certainly did not have to be filled with the problems of trash disposal! And he should be clutching at each available minute. He had hoped . . .

He did deplore the interruption which Amy's death had made in his personal time. Today, instead of being on duty, setting bones, seeing postoperative patients, instructing his interns, he had had to attend to the details conceding that unfortunate death. And tonight, instead of sweating over his plans for the future, he was on duty —

He hadn't even time to think about this interruption in his plans. He must sign charts, check on tractions . . .

The Boards had come up during the previous weekend, and what seemed to be Eric Ritter's whole future had depended on his passing those stiff examinations. Written ones, oral ones. He had had to study, he had had to get his knowledge and experience lined up in an orderly fashion . . .

Tim Dineen had given him a whole afternoon and evening to help him prepare for the exams. Dineen had been through the mill. He had taken and passed the Boards, and had come out a Fellow in Orthopedic Surgery. Eric's specialty was spinal surgery, but it was the Ortho Boards which he had needed to pass. He had been doing the work, and studying, for four years. Tim's help had been valuable.

And now, in spite of his wife's death, he would get in touch with Eric. And of course he would come back to get Nancy Colburn out of jail. Of all damfool, ridiculous things to do! Eric himself, once freed of this thirty-six-hour duty, would put some time into getting that mess straightened out!

How could anyone get an idea that Nancy had killed Amy? How could they think she would ever do such a thing? The death was a suicide, plain and simple. No, he didn't know the weapon used, but Grampa told him that, months ago, Amy had broken a glass and threatened to cut her throat! This would establish a pattern of suicidal intent. Eric had told the coroner that it was suicide! What price his medical training if he could not determine a thing like that?

Amy had threatened to try the thing again. Grampa's testimony might not be taken seriously — he was old, and perhaps he was senile. But others in the hotel would remember. They'd hushed up the first episode. Resort hotels had to be careful about such stories getting about; they wished today's event could be put into a box and forgotten.

But it was not to be ignored, not at Nancy's expense! No, sireee! Not if Eric could prevent it. He —

Just then his bleeper summoned him to Emergency where an "unruly" patient had been admitted. And the patient most certainly was unruly. Swearing, shouting, throwing himself about. He had been picked up on the Interstate, drunk. There were abrasions, as if he'd been thrown or had jumped from a car. It was almost impossible to examine him. X-rays wouldn't be any good, though there could be fractures.

Even the emergency room crew decided that they had never heard such foul language.

Dr. Ritter prescribed 15 cc.'s of paraldehyde and bed rest for twelve hours. "Under restraint," he added as he left e.r. "Clean up the abrasions after he has quieted. I'll see him in the morning."

"*Whooosh!*" he told himself as he went swiftly down the hall. He would make rounds, then settle down for an hour of plan making. He would pray for a quiet night. Pray hard!

He did make the rounds, he did go to his room, turned on the lamp, and propped his feet on the end of his bed. And he yawned. Good Lord! This was not the night for him to be sleepy! He picked up a journal, read a paragraph, began a second. His eyes blurred. He jumped to his feet, dashed cold water on his face, and reached for the towel.

Did Gayle know that Nancy had been taken downtown and held for questioning? Her parents would know, and they would be terribly upset. Eric should go to the house and reassure them. But he couldn't do even humane things, he could not leave the hospital until day after tomorrow. By then —

He sat down again, and the phone buzzed.

Would he come down to X-ray, please?

He sighed, and said, yes, he would. He supposed there was a difficulty . . .

And there was. The head technologist, a fine one, who had been doing his work since Eric could remember, which was before he'd entered medical school, was being confronted by an irate man who seemed to be demanding that Busekist be fired.

Eric laughed. "We can't fire a technician as good as Mr. Busekist, sir," he said. "What seems to be the trouble?"

The man sputtered, and soon Busekist was sputtering, too. It took Eric nearly a half hour to get things straightened out. The man's wife, it seemed, had five days previously entered the hospital with pneumonitis. There was a first hurdle to be cleared there, because the patient confused the illness with pneumonia, and was, through self-diagnosis, sure there was something terribly wrong with herself. Tb, at least. She was so *sore* . . .

Eric found himself engaging on a medical lecture concerning the lungs, viral infections — He broke off. "Why does the gentleman want you fired, Busekist?" he asked.

The patient's husband answered him. Chest X-rays had been ordered . . .

"That's routine," said the tall, handsome,

and young doctor.

"I took the pictures," said Busekist. "I have the plates here, Doctor. They showed nothing. I still can't find a thing!"

This statement appeared to infuriate their man. By God, he declared, pictures would be taken until they *did* find something!

Eric studied him. Would he like, he asked quietly, for Dr. Ritter to examine his wife?

Not if he was an intern.

"I'll look at the chart," said Eric. He turned off the viewing light, he lifted a finger to the technologist and advised him to go home and rest. "Why are you here at this hour, anyway?" he asked. "This couldn't have been an emergency call."

"I am afraid it was one," said the patient's husband.

Eric decided that he should continue his lecture. The man's wife, he said, had had an inflammation of her lung. Evidently there was no lesion. That was why the picture showed none —

He could only half solve the problem. The patient would go home the next day, her side still hurting. With rest and medication she should be much better in a week.

And Busekist would not be fired!

"But I'll continue to be called an intern," Eric told himself wryly.

"We'll laugh about this by the middle of the week," said Busekist ten minutes later when Eric met him in the hall.

"Not me," said the Resident. "I was hoping for a quiet night."

"Yes, sir. I heard you got pulled into that thing at the hotel. Is Dr. Dineen still in town?"

"I don't know," said Eric. "I'd like to see him if he is."

He went back to the surgical floor, his mind swirling. Did Tim know about Nancy's being . . . ? He'd be upset. He seemed to be very fond of Gayle's younger sister. So was Eric, fond of Nancy. She was a darling girl! She —

Eric groaned. Doctoring didn't leave a man chance to be human! He should phone Nancy's parents. He should locate Tim Dineen. He should be attending to his own personal affairs.

And so the night seemed to be going. A woman on Medical died because her attending doctor had discontinued giving her fluids after weeks of diarrhea and i.v.'s. The medical resident was calling it a mercy killing; the patient might have lived a couple of weeks more with fluids.

On that particular night, Eric did not want to discuss mercy killings. But he did let

118

the medical resident talk about it. These situations got into a doctor's craw, and had to be resolved some way.

Next, after a half hour of being free, one of his own patients stirred up a crisis. Poor thing. She was dying of cancer, and her problem was the continuous, intractable pain. The cancer had invaded both breasts, then an ovary, all three subject to surgery. But lately it had shown up in a vertebra, and morphine was no longer touching the pain which came in great, sweeping spasms. The young woman's personality was being broken down. A chordotomy seemed to be the only solution. But the staff surgeon would have to order that. And Eric must decide if the decision could be made a part of tonight's schedule.

He just wished all the people who glibly condemned mercy killing could know a six-hour nursing tour of patients like the woman down on Medical, or his cancer of the spine case up here on Surgical.

Or Amy Dineen, blind, hopeless, young . . .

Tim Dineen definitely was still in Peter's Beach. About eight o'clock he ate dinner in his room at the hotel, and the waiter was the one to tell him that Nancy Colburn was being held by the police. "Do *you* think she killed your wife, Doctor?"

Tim stared at the man. "Who started such a story?" he asked.

The waiter shrugged. "I just know that someone was saying that Miss Gayle's sister . . ."

Was *Gayle* saying it? She could. Maybe. Not really meaning to get Nancy into trouble. But Gayle lived on excitement and sensationalism. She —

"I'll look into the matter," he told the waiter. "Are you sure they took Miss Nancy to *jail?*"

"I jes know what's bein' told, Doctor."

"All right, all right."

He would talk to people who would know. Not Gayle. He'd stay clear of *her!*

He finished his dinner, and never could remember what he had eaten.

He went downstairs and talked to various people at the hotel. Mr. Parmeley, the manager — He called the hospital, but Dr. Ritter was with a patient. He called the newspaper office, and confirmed that Nancy was being held.

He cursed the poor guy who had given him the information. And then apologized. "But the whole thing is ridiculous!" he explained. "Who filed charges? Do you know?"

"We just got the word, Dr. Dineen, that the District Attorney's office was holding Nancy Colburn for questioning."

"*Where* are they holding her?"

"I think . . ."

"In the police lockup?" With weekend drunks and junkheads?

"Our information is, sir, that she is being held in the city jail."

Tim hung up. He must talk to a dozen people at once. The D.A. Nancy, herself — He tried Eric again. Dr. Ritter was not free.

Tim decided to go down the road and talk to Nancy's parents. He looked at his watch. Eight-thirty. He sighed deeply, and struck out.

He passed people without seeing them, he heard the ocean's pulse and thought no more of it than he did of the moonlight and the soft breeze against his face.

He was thinking of Nancy as she had talked to him that afternoon, her pale hair in fine wisps clinging to her soft cheek, her soft lips trembling and her gray eyes darkened with pity for him and for Amy.

He crossed the patio of the Colburn home, went to the front door and touched the bell. There were lights, the family was still up and alert. Gayle, even, might be there. Though he hoped not.

Dr. Colburn opened the door and invited Dr. Dineen to come in. His manner was restrained and courteous. "My wife is in the Living room . . ." he said, leading the way.

Tim went swiftly to her, urging her not to rise.

But she held her hands out to him. "Tim, dear," she said. "We should have come to you."

"Not at all." He sat down beside her. Dr. Colburn stood before the fireplace, his manner reserved and watchful.

"I heard, less than an hour ago," Tim said quickly, "that the authorities have questioned Nancy about Amy's death."

"Only because she was probably the last one to see her," explained Nancy's mother. "She couldn't have done anything, Tim! They'll decide that, and bring her back."

Tim glanced at Nancy's father.

"It's been a bad day," he said. "For all of us. You, too, Tim."

"Yes, sir. Of course it has. But — Did they really come here and take Nancy downtown?"

"Oh, yes, they did, Tim. They did indeed."

"Well, I hope you know that I made no charges against her!"

"We do know that. But it seems — Well,

they are holding her."

"We'll get a lawyer and have her out of this! We —"

Dr. Colburn took a step forward. "I got a lawyer, Tim," he said. "Heser. You may want your own."

"Why?" asked Tim. "I'm on your side. I *know* that Nancy did nothing to hurt Amy! Eric said it was suicide. What do the police thing they are doing?"

Dr. Colburn's mouth twisted wryly. "They are protecting this county against dangerous people like our hundred-and-five-pound girl!" he said bitterly.

Tim stood up. "I'll get this straightened out," he promised. "I'll go downtown myself. I'll pick Eric up and take him with me."

Dr. Colburn shrugged. "I wish you luck," he said.

"You don't think . . . ?"

"I don't know what to think, Tim. I've never been into a thing like this. Heser assures me that Nancy is safe —"

"She's in *jail!*"

"Yes, she is, and we none of us like that. Especially Nancy, I should think. They are holding her for questioning by the grand jury. The case is called 'suspected homicide,' but without formal charges being made. That Eskridge fellow — You know

123

him? He's in the District Attorney's office."

"This is all new to me, too, sir."

"Er — yes. I presume it is."

"Does Mr. Heser know that I don't believe — ?"

You could tell him. I told him *I* didn't believe it, and it made no difference. Nancy told him that she was innocent . . ."

"Well, of course she is innocent! I'll talk to him. I'll pick up Eric and we'll go to see Nancy — Isn't there something called *habeas corpus?*"

"I hope we still have such a thing," said Dr. Colburn. He sounded very tired.

Tim went across to him. "Don't worry, sir. We'll get things done. If I don't think Nancy could kill anybody —"

"They might think you were behind her doing it," said Veronica Colburn unexpectedly.

The men turned sharply. The slender, quiet scholar, the young, broad-shouldered doctor — Their mouths fell open in astonishment.

"Mother . . ." protested Andrew Colburn.

"I read a lot of mystery — detective — stories," she argued. "I don't say Tim or Nancy would contrive to do such a terrible thing! But I do say the police are going to suspect that they did."

Tim took his handkerchief from his jacket pocket. "I'd better get busy while I'm still free," he said weakly. "Dr. Colburn, you'd better get some sleep. And Mrs. Colburn, too. Could I suggest a sedative?"

Nancy's father came to him, took his arm. "We'll take care of ourselves," he said. "You do what you can. But don't forget; it's Saturday night, tomorrow is Sunday, and —"

Tim left, going first to the hospital rather than to the hotel for his car. He would talk to Eric, persuade him — though Ritter would not need persuading. He'd *want* to help Nancy!

Eric did want to. He agreed with Tim that the whole situation was a nightmare. "And I thought I'd have some time to concentrate on my own affairs," he admitted. "Though I'd help you, Tim. It's just that a resident on duty . . ."

Tim nodded. The sky could fall, and the ocean roll back . . . "Don't worry," he said. "I'll do everything I can think of. In a day or two you and I will be talking about those Boards." He did not think he should mention Mrs. Colburn's solution to the mystery of the arrest.

He did talk to Mr. Heser, who also reminded him that it was Saturday night.

"I am still going to see Nancy," Tim assured him.

"You probably won't make it, Dr. Dineen."

"I have to try."

"I'll see her myself, tomorrow."

"I want to tell her in person that I don't think she should be held. How is she anyway?"

Mr. Heser rubbed the back of his neck. "Well, she was shocked, of course. But she held up pretty well. There's just one thing . . ."

Tim turned. "What one thing?" he asked sharply.

"She cannot accept the fact that what she says as the truth cannot be believed."

Tim sighed. "I can't accept that, either," he confessed. "Other women, maybe. But not Nancy. Never Nancy."

He stood looking at the lawyer. Heser had a youthful appearance. He was not as young as he appeared to be, and he had a very good reputation in the district. He was a successful man.

"Tell me," said Tim urgently. "One more thing. How did this fool thing ever get started?" If Heser mentioned Gayle, Tim would go, personally, and shake the truth out of that girl, that —

"I think the nurse is behind this investigation," Heser was saying. "If I should have any defending to do, that would be my line of straightening all this out. I think the nurse feared she might be blamed."

Tim considered that. "You could be right," he agreed. "Even though Dr. Ritter certified the death as suicide."

"I understand the nurse testified that Mrs. Dineen could not have cut her wrist, that she had no use of her hands."

Tim looked surprised. "But she did have!" he protested. "Not a lot, but the nurse should know that she could use them."

"We'll try to break down her testimony in various ways, Doctor."

"If we need to. I'm going over to see Nancy now."

Heser still looked doubtful. "Well, good luck!" he said as he closed his front door.

Tim did not see Nancy that night. He tried. At the city jail he told the desk sergeant that he had come to see Miss Colburn. "I understand that, through a mistake, you are holding her here."

"Yes, sir," said the man politely.

Tim took out his wallet and showed his identification cards. "I am the husband of the woman in the case with which Miss Colburn has been connected. Nobody killed my wife, and I want to get things straightened out so that she can go home."

The sergeant studied the cards, he looked up into Tim's face. "I'm sorry, sir. I have no authority to do anything to help you."

"But who in hell does have that authority?" Tim shouted.

The policeman seated at a second desk looked around.

"Can't I *see* her?" Tim asked.

"No, sir."

"But why not?"

"Regulations, sir. No visitors to any inmate at this hour. And we have orders . . ."

Tim said, specifically, what he thought of the man's orders. He became more angry and more excited. He shouted. The sergeant stood up.

"Look, Doctor. We don't want to have to arrest you for creating a disturbance. Miss Colburn is all right. You'd best go home. Perhaps tomorrow, or Monday, you could get a court order. For tonight — you've had a hard day."

Tim stepped back. He had indeed had a hard day.

"We are sorry your wife died, sir."

"Yes. So am I. Of course she could have died at any time. That's what I can't understand, Sergeant. Why do they say anyone *murdered* her? It's completely nonsense."

The sergeant nodded, even as he answered the telephone. "We'll send someone right out," he said into the mouthpiece. He pushed buttons and told the dispatcher to send a squad car to a certain drugstore — probable holdup and robbery.

He turned back to Tim. "Saturday nights get busy, Doctor," he said kindly. "Drug holdups, family rows. Now, like I say, you get some rest. I don't have any authority to help you. Miss Colburn is all right. We'll keep her here and —"

"For how long will you keep her?"

"She's held for questioning, sir. Maybe she will be kept until the grand jury can hold a hearing."

"But —"

"You could talk to her lawyer. The grand jury decides if there is a case, then charges are filed and a trial date set."

"And I can't see her?"

"No, sir. Not tonight. That's the way these things go, Dr. Dineen."

Tim looked around the office. He stood uncertain, then went out. The two officers watched him go.

"Who do you think done it?" asked the younger man.

The sergeant reached for the ringing phone. "In this job," he said, "I don't get paid to think."

During that long, strange night on the cot in the jail cell, Nancy would have claimed that she did not sleep at all. She said this to Mr. Heser when he came to see her.

"My patients often told me that," she said, "and I never would believe them."

He smiled and nodded. "How are you?"

She shrugged. She had combed her hair, and, she said, had eaten breakfast. "They bring my food to me."

"Good. What did you have?"

"Coffee and oatmeal. Not good, but not really bad. I mopped my room — my cell — and made my bed. I don't see a lot of people, but I *hear* a lot of them."

"Yes. Now, Nancy, I'm afraid we can't accomplish much today. It's Sunday, you know." He told about Tim's coming to his home. He had talked to Nancy's father. He explained what was meant by her being held for the grand jury's questioning. He saw the girl pale.

"It may not be at all bad," he said quickly.

"How many people will be there?"

"How many? Oh, maybe twenty. It won't be a public hearing. The jury, and the

130

people who were present last night."

"Three or four," Nancy agreed. "I — that wasn't easy, but I handled it."

"Yes, you did. And you will handle . . ."

"Mr. Heser, I *wish* I didn't have to face them! Twenty people looking at me, not believing — not liking me."

"Oh, now, Nancy."

"If they liked me they wouldn't think I could do — what they say I did." She stared down at her hands.

He did his best to reassure her. He had brought her a book to read.

She looked up at him. "Thank you for the book," she said. "Could I — Do you think I could have some paper and a pencil?"

"Why, yes, I should think so." He opened his briefcase and found a small pad of white paper. He took a ball-point pen from his pocket.

"They wouldn't give me any paper last night," she told him shyly.

"I can't imagine why not. But I'll tell them I've given the things to you. We don't want any complications, do we?"

She managed a smile. "No, indeed," she said.

"Are you going to write a book of your own?"

He was trying to cheer her up. She answered seriously. "I am going to chart out," she said, "everything that's happened to put me here. There must be some reason . . ."

He nodded. Maybe she, too, would reach the conclusions that Dr. Dineen and Nancy's attorney had attained the night before.

"I didn't do it!" she said firmly when he left her. "If you are going to church, please pray that I am believed."

He was shaking his head as he went down the corridor. A man in one of the cells was singing softly to himself. *"You gotta walk that lonesome road . . ."*

Nancy heard the man singing, she heard Arthur Heser's footsteps go down the corridor, she heard the barred gate open and close . . .

She sat on the stool and smoothed her hand over the top page of the tablet which he had given her. She looked up at the window, a triangle of sunlight came through it, and a flying bird crossed that triangle.

She had said she would go back and chart out — but where should she start? She would make notes, and try to figure out how she had got where she was, what had happened. Doctors did that with patients. They took a detailed history, they asked questions, put the answers down, considered them all, and came to a conclusion, a diagnosis. Then would follow the recommendations for improving the situation. Medicine, therapy, surgery . . .

Dr. Dineen did that with his patients, and a cure often resulted. Certainly progress was to be expected.

So — Could Nancy follow that course? Beginning when? She need not go back to childhood measles or rheumatic fever. But when had things changed for her? Begun to change?

Everything had been just super when she was in the city, busy at the hospital. Morning surgery, post-ops, intensive care — emergency surgery. Set things up, see the patient, change clothes, scrub — prep —

Things had been just grand then. Oh, her back would ache, and her feet swell . . .

"What are you grinning about, Colburn?"

"Because I'm going on vacation as of five o'clock tonight!"

"Whatever will all the sick folks do?"

"I don't know. But I know what I'll do."

"Sleep, eat, and get fat."

"No, *sir!* Because I'll also swim, and swim, and *swim!*"

Yes. Things had been all right for Nancy then. She had been busy, happy, and liked by her friends.

Chapter 5

Nancy had indeed come home. Two weeks ago, she had come, planning on a better than two-week vacation. A rest, recreation, and sunshine. She had looked forward to it, planned on it. And talked about it, she supposed. Dr. Dineen had heard of it, and right there in o.r. one morning, he had offered to drive her. "I'm going down to the Beach on Friday."

This was kind of him, and not unusual. He went to the Beach, usually about three times a month. It was known that he served as orthopedic consultant for the hospital there. But Nancy took a little good-natured teasing about the publicity of his offer.

She had been glad to drive down with Tim. Someday she would buy her own car, but had not, so far. That afternoon they had talked — about the hospital, about the Beach. What she would do on her vacation.

"Drop in on Amy a time or two," he had suggested. "I'm sure it relieves the monotony."

Since she always did go to see Amy, she

had agreed as a matter of course. He'd dropped her at her parents' home, and had visited with them for a few minutes. And after two weeks, he had come again, his week, to the Beach. Nancy had seen him, she had watched a parade . . .

And now . . .

She straightened her back, and her thoughts. Two weeks ago she had come to Peter's Beach for a vacation.

Yes.

And it spite of herself, she thought back to the hospital again. Which was all right. She should determine the firm background of her work there. She liked that work, and her life. Because of Tim's guidance, she had acquired a good education as well as a solid profession. She worked hard but could have pride in that work. She liked what she did, and the people with whom she worked. They seemed to like her. More and more often the other staff doctors were asking for her to be assigned to their o.r.'s. Tim did, often.

Gazing up at the shifting patch of sunlight, Nancy smiled wistfully to remember the work which Tim did. Just to see him in o.r. Big, quiet, able. To watch him care for the club feet of a tiny baby, coming back again for the cast changes, and again — Not his most spectacular surgery, but one that was typical, and that satisfied. Before her own vacation was over, Nancy had found herself missing her work. Though she did enjoy being at home, talking to her mother and dad. Buying summer clothes. A tennis dress, the pretty blue arid green voile, two swimsuits. Denim shorts, a nubbly white linen skirt. Blouses and bright sandals.

Almost at once she had gone to the Beach, and was down there two or three times each day. One rainy day, she had wrapped up and walked along the edge of the swift, hissing waves.

She had seen her friends, some of them young mothers with enchanting babies. There were picnics on the beach — bronze-bodied young men, girls with flying hair. Wild beach hats and chunks of early watermelon eaten after thin steaks quickly broiled over an open fire. Talk, singing, laughter. A good vacation. Her friends had been glad to see her, they seemed to like her.

There had been a few things to color, to scratch, even to mar the beauty of those sixteen days. But not through any fault of Nancy's. Not because she had made a mistake or a blunder. Certainly not because she had set out to harm anyone.

First, her father had suggested that she

could work at the Beach hospital, and live at home. She thought that she did not want to make the change.

Then — Gayle thought that she should come to her shop for clothes. Nancy thought she could not afford them. "I don't need really fancy things, Gayle."

"Not *fancy* . . ."

"The prices are, on my budget." Gayle had made a face at the word.

And then, though actually only four days after her arrival, there was the party. A party which her mother had been planning and arranging for days, maybe weeks, before Nancy's arrival. This frightened her at first. Surely not a party for *her?*

No. It seemed not. Her mother had had the house cleaned and furbished. She had brought out silver and china and crystal; she had rewashed and ironed stacks of small, embroidered napkins, and had already baked dozens of tiny cakes, planned just as many sandwiches. Nancy could help her there, though she must be sure to have a dress, and get her hair done . . .

"Wait a minute, Mother!" Nancy had protested. "What's going on here?"

"I want flowers for the house, but I want the garden pretty, too," Mrs. Colburn had continued on momentum. "Oh, Nancy!

Why, it's a party, a tea, to announce Gayle's engagement. My friends are invited from three to four, yours and Gayle's from four-thirty to six."

"And we get leftovers for dinner," declared Dr Colburn.

Nancy smiled at him. Gayle's engagement to whom? There had been so many men, so many before this —

"Why, it's Eric, dear. I wanted Gayle to tell you but she's so high in the clouds . . ."

Now, two weeks later, Nancy didn't remember what she had said. Nothing too wrong evidently.

And she had not needed to say anything to Gayle just then. Not until the buzzing in her head had stopped, not until the cold feeling of loss and sadness was swallowed.

But — *Eric* and Gayle?

Of course, the rich man's son, handsome, charming — every girl and woman had tried to catch Eric Ritter. But what about the *doctor?* Eric had worked hard at his profession. In a week he was to face the specialist examinations. Would Gayle . . . ?

"How soon?" she remembered saying hoarsely.

"In six weeks. Eric is taking some sort of position in England. They will honeymoon . . ."

Again Nancy had felt as if she were sinking into deep water, her hands tied against any effort to save herself. Or Eric.

Jealousy. That was what engulfed her again now. Green, sour jealousy. She was ashamed. But how could she endure seeing Gayle marry the big, golden-haired man whom Nancy had loved truly, physically loved, long before she was old enough to have his money matter to her? Ever since he had come to live at the hotel with his grandparents. He was much older than Nancy. Eight years older. When she was sixteen, Eric had been a medical student, golden and laughing. He'd taught her how to sail his Sunfish. In all ways he'd been grand to her. He seemed everything desirable which a man could be. And, someday, she dreamed . . .

But now, Gayle . . .

She could not believe this. And yet she had to believe it. She had to face the fact that she had seen this possibility developing. On her visits home, she had seen Eric and Gayle together. Dancing at the hotel last winter . . . Their parents had taken the girls to dinner at the hotel for a special affair. Gayle had worn a really lovely red silk dress. Her face was vivid and lovely — radiant. There was an orchestra; Eric had come in, and to their table. And he had asked Gayle to dance.

Nancy had watched them, then not willing to see, but now remembering, Eric's blind, adoring manner with her sister. So she was ready to accept her mother's opinion of two weeks ago that Eric was crazy about Gayle.

Though for her sister to marry a doctor still did not seem right to Nancy, not right at all. Nancy knew Gayle, and she knew Eric. She could understand her sister, but for Eric, she was puzzled. She wished she could talk about it to Tim Dineen. Or maybe to Grampa.

She knew Grampa about as well as she knew her own father. All her life Nancy had done what her mother called "hanging around the hotel." She guessed she had.

She had used the beach, she'd gone into the hotel for all sorts of reasons — stamps, to use the telephone, to buy Lifesavers . . .

"It's not like other hotels," Dr. Colburn had reassured Nancy's mother. "I myself feel like one of the family."

So did Nancy. So did the Ritters. On this present vacation — two days after her arrival, the Colburns had gone to the hotel for Sunday dinner. Eric had been there with his father's sister, Frances Parmeley, her husband Eugene and their four children. Grampa sat at the head of the table. This last year, Grampa had failed some. But the kids were full of vim and vigor. Eugene Parmeley, her dad had told her, was acting as manager of the hotel. At least until Grampa recovered from the shock of Grandma's death.

Eric came over and spoke to the Colburns. "Where's Gayle?" he had asked.

"You may as well get used to it," said Dr. Colburn. "Gayle sleeps all day every Sunday."

"Get used to it, or find a way to make her do differently," said Gayle's mother.

Eric had chatted with them for several minutes while Nancy studied him. The way his thick eyelashes grew clear to the corners of his eyes, the way a small dimple could faintly shadow one cheek.

"I cannot feature Gayle's marrying a doctor," she blurted out when Eric left them.

"As a matter of fact, neither can I," said Dr. Colburn. "Not the sort of doctor Eric is."

"Is he different from other doctors?" asked Veronica Colburn.

Both her husband and Nancy answered her. She dismissed Nancy's opinion. "You've

141

had a crush on Eric as long as you've known him," she had said.

"I know it," Nancy agreed. "And I'm hoping he'll succeed in his profession. I believe it will be harder for a rich young man."

"He'll make it," said her father. "He works hard, and knows what he is going for."

Gayle. Nancy's thoughts had whispered to her.

Chapter 6

Nancy now sat, her chin in her hand, thinking deeply. She completely forgot where she was, why she was in the city jail. Gradually Gayle faded out of the picture, and she thought only about the Ritters. They were a special part of her life. All mixed up with the crystal chandeliers and the curving grand stairway of the hotel, the great kitchen where the white-hatted cooks worked in a constant aura of steam and heat and strangely exciting scents, was the family. The Ritters.

Special people. They had always seemed to be. They still were.

On her first Sunday of this vacation her father had taken his family to the hotel for dinner. This was a ritual thing to do. Nancy had worn a white linen suit with a flaming red blouse. Her mother had not exactly approved of the outfit for church, but when he came to their table, Eric said that he admired it.

And he asked about Gayle.

"I'm with the family," he had explained unnecessarily. Nancy could see them now, as in a photograph. Grampa, as clean as a new whistle, trying not to show how much he missed Grandma. Frances, sister to Eric's father, dead in the Second War, now sat in Grandma's place. Frances did not look at all well, and Nancy's mother said that she had been sick. "I think she had surgery of some kind."

Her husband, Eugene Parmeley, was there, and in Nancy's photograph were, of course, the four Parmeley children. The family grandchildren. Barbara, a college student, a slight girl, very dark, with the long, hanging, straight hair so many girls still wore. Nancy had seen her in Gayle's shop the day before.

Laurel, about twelve, was blonde, like Eric. There were two little boys about ten and eight. Greg II and Arthur. His family made a tableful, she told Eric.

"Yes, it does. And we use a lot of catsup."

Laughing, he rejoined that family.

Nancy watched him go, she watched him at the table, among his own people. Her mother and father were talking — about Eric, she realized with a start. Her father was laughing and saying that if he went to London he would need to learn to pronounce the word "med-cin" the way the English did.

She looked up. "Is he really going?" she said.

"If he passes the exams creditably."

"Oh, he'll pass them."

"I believe he wants to do it so well that he will be given some sort of honorable degree."

"Diplomate," murmured Nancy. *What did Gayle know about diplomates, fellows, and certifications?* For that matter, what did she care?

"He's worried because he has specialized in such a narrow field," Dr. Colburn was explaining. "He talked to me about it one night when Gayle kept him waiting to go somewhere."

"I'll bet she did," thought Nancy.

"It seems," lectured the scholar, "that Eric has completed four pieces of original research, and has had papers published on them."

Nancy's attention brightened. "Has he really, Dad?"

"Yes, he told me. They concerned, largely, the spinal ganglia and the spinal cord."

Nancy leaned toward him. "On humans, Dad? He's done that on people?"

"No," said her father. "On crayfish."

Nancy smiled and nodded. "That figures," she said. "But do you really suppose

Eric talks to Gayle about such things?"

Her parents laughed and said probably he did not.

"But Eric's a fine doctor," Andrew Colburn insisted. "He's done four residencies, and his family is very proud of him."

"If he's really good," Nancy agreed, "they should be."

"I don't suppose they know any more about his being good than I do," said her father. "He could be the very best. Though of course he has been raised spoiled, and that too often means that he has not worked to his full ability. As a teacher, I know that happens. He —"

He broke off to get to his feet; friends had stopped at their table to speak to the Colburns, to welcome Nancy home, and to ask about Gayle.

"She isn't with you . . ." said Mrs. Monroe.

Obviously she was not. Gayle had not gone to church either, where these same people had sat across the aisle from the Colburns. Nancy ate her shrimp, and watched Eric.

Departing, Mrs. Monroe patted her shoulder. "Still mooning about Eric, Nancy?" she asked archly. "I remember, when you were fifteen, you had such a crush on that boy."

"I still do," Nancy agreed. "It doesn't get me anywhere now, either."

She ate the rest of the shrimp, and thought about Eric, when she was sixteen, and since. From the first he had seemed a romantic figure. Not only that he was handsome, but then he was lately an orphan. His mother had died and he had come to live with Grampa. People older and wiser than young Nancy had watched the boy and wondered how he would turn out. Even then he had not been exactly a *boy*. Rather, a medical student who came to the hotel for vacations. He and Nancy Colburn had swum a lot together, and sailed. It was highly possible that he had used the skinny little blonde girl as a baffle against all the more determined young women. The most adult joke Nancy could remember between the two of them had been summer-long laughter at the way the expanding hospital was bragging about its "Forty more private and semi-private beds."

But it had been fun.

And for years Nancy had been accumulating her pictures of the assembled Ritter family eating Sunday dinner in the big dining room. Grampa greeting their friends and guests. The little children sometimes misbehaved. Grandma never wanted them punished, but she sternly reprimanded Grampa when he told about once being arrested in Amarillo.

She thought he should set a better example.

"I was only going eight miles over the limit," Grampa had said. "And they never would have made me go to the station if I hadn't been driving a Cadillac."

"In *Texas?*" Eric had protested. "In Texas, Cadillacs are more common than bicycles."

"Don't have bicycles because they don't have sidewalks!" Grampa instructed him.

Nancy repeated this story, heard many times, that Sunday when she and her parents, without Gayle, had eaten dinner at the hotel.

"Poor Grandma," she murmured now, remembering.

That day, too — "I'll bet Gayle finds Eric's research with crayfish fascinating," had drawled Nancy, savoring her minted iced tea.

And of course her mother had reproved her. It was not good for sisters to criticize or be jealous. Nancy would find a good man, and marry him. "Will you make sandwiches with black walnuts and cream cheese?" she asked. "To announce my engagement?"

And, this morning, two weeks later, with

the sounds of some sort of church service going on down the long corridor of the jail, Nancy wept to remember her impudence.

That other Sunday, the one of two weeks ago, she had apologized to her mother and asked for particulars about Grandma's death.

"But you've been home since then," her mother had said.

"I know, but never for more than a day or two. Even at Christmas. I heard only that Mrs. Ritter was in the hospital, but you didn't think I should go to see her. And the next thing I knew, she was dead."

"Yes. She died in February. The family had a private funeral, and didn't talk much about her illness, so I suspect it was cancer."

"Why?" asked Nancy, professionally curious.

"Oh, people never want to talk about cancer. And of course, because of the hotel, the funeral had to be quiet. But poor Grampa never got over her death. Some say he has become quite childish."

"I don't get that impression," said Nancy. "He's old, of course, but he keeps himself as neat as a pin, sits in the lobby, the way he's done for years, and talks to people."

"I know," agreed her mother. "But there are things — For instance . . ."

"Now, Mother," said Dr. Colburn warningly.

"Well, she'll hear it, Andrew!" Her mother turned back to Nancy. "My dear, there is constant talk about Grampa marrying again."

"Marrying who?" She glanced at her father. "Whom," she corrected herself, smiling at him.

He nodded. "They can revise the Bible, the Prayer Book, fairy tales — and grammar," he agreed. "But I'll be no party to any of it!"

"Good for you!" Nancy applauded him. "As for Grampa . . . Do I know any of the prospects?"

"Just about every unattached female in town. Someone even had the audacity to mention Gayle."

"Is that why you are announcing her engagement to Eric?" Nancy asked.

"I don't take such talk seriously," said her mother.

"Then you shouldn't repeat it seriously," said her husband firmly. "But I will tell you, Nancy, that even ridiculous gossip does keep the Ritter relatives on the hot seat."

Nancy laughed delightedly. "It must, to get you to use slang."

She looked across the big dining room at

the Ritter table. "What sort of job does Mr. Parmeley do of managing the hotel?" she asked.

"All right, I think."

"With Grampa to check on him."

Her father had smiled faintly and asked "the ladies" if they wanted dessert.

That had been two weeks ago.

Chapter 7

Nancy wrote busily on her tablet, knowing where she was, keenly feeling the present circumstances, and at the same time transported to other places and other times.

Again she stared off into space. She had thought about Eric, and her parents — about the hotel . . . Now she should really think about Tim Dineen. And, of course, that meant Amy. And Gayle again.

Oh, dear. How could she be jealous of Gayle's relationship to *two* men? Well, she could. Because she honestly believed that while Gayle might be planning to marry Eric, she did love Tim.

When he first had come to the Beach, she had fallen hard for him, and just — last night? No, Friday night. Before it was dark, Nancy had seen them together on the beach. Talking earnestly. Of course not touching one another, but they had talked! That was before Amy was found . . .

Nancy rose and, using the tin cup, got herself a drink of water. She walked around the room — the cell — and thought about

Tim and Gayle. She remembered just the way he looked, how he had been, when first he had come to the hotel. She could remember every single thing he had done and every word he had said to her. He had built her life; that was what he had done!

And she would always be grateful, she always would thank him. Yes, and love him.

Though not as she loved Eric, with excitement, chills and thrills. And Gayle's feeling for him was not what she now claimed to have for Eric. But back then, seven years ago, Nancy had watched them. And the thrills were there.

Gayle, at eighteen, had chattered to her young sister about the wonderful man who had come to the hotel. She described her thrills, she told everything Tim had said, each look, each touch. Nancy, fifteen, had listened with envy.

At eighteen Gayle had been a beautiful young girl, with shining brown hair, an excited welcome for life in her bright eyes and her laughter. This was the first *man* she had ever known "this way," she told Nancy. A real man. She could just *die* when he touched her or even spoke to her . . .

Nancy remembered. She remembered how Tim had been then, though not so different from the older man he was now. Now he was a year or two beyond thirty-five. And looked little older than when he first brought Amy to the hotel, and first sought out Gayle for diversion. Physically fit, he had high cheekbones set in a sharp-featured, clean-skinned face. His dark hair then was cut somewhat shorter to his head. He had a large, strong nose, dark, keen eyes. Steady eyes.

He and Gayle . . .

That first summer he had come often to the Beach to be sure that his wife was comfortably settled. And each time he came, he had "seen" Gayle. Sometimes coming to the house, sometimes . . .

Now, searingly, and through much thinking about it, Nancy remembered one particular night. There had been some sort of picnic for the high school crowd. It had started on the hotel beach, with food in hampers, and the usual loud talk, singing, horseplay. When dark came and things got chilly, the young people had gone up to the hotel coffee shop for Cokes and Berliners, a fad with them just then. And during that hour, Nancy realized that she had left her beach bag back on the sand. Without saying anything to anyone, she had run back to retrieve it. She had come around the lifeguard tower, and almost stepped on a man and a girl, deeply embraced, deeply unconscious of where they were, aware only of what they were doing. The girl was Gayle, her sister. The man — the new doctor whose invalid wife lived at the hotel.

Nancy had backed away, shocked at what she had seen . . .

She was almost sixteen, and no dummy. Seven years ago the facts of life were a part of any adolescent's education. Her parents, her school, the talk of her peers, movies and books had given her explicit information. What shocked her that night was her sister's involvement. She did not want that to happen to Gayle any more than she would want it to happen to herself.

It worried her, it shamed her. And one day she talked to her mother about the new doctor. Gayle thought he was very nice, she said.

"He is nice, Nancy. Poor man."

The term had surprised Nancy.

"Because of his wife," explained Mrs. Colburn. She'd been rolling out piecrust. "A young man needs a woman to love, and this young man's wife . . ." She shook her head and fitted the round of pastry into a shiny pan.

"What," had asked the young girl, "what if he finds other girls to love?"

"He may do that," agreed her mother. "Hand me the cinnamon, dear. But I don't think Dr. Dineen is the sort to do a lot of it. The right girl might catch him at the right time, and he might step over. But he knows as well as anyone — better, I suspect — that he cannot marry any girl to whom he might honestly be attracted."

"But —"

"The girl should know that, too. She should know exactly what she is doing."

Had her mother suspected that Nancy was talking about Gayle? She could have. Veronica Colburn was no fool. That morning, seven years ago, she had continued to make her pie, and she had talked some more to Nancy about Tim and Amy Dineen.

They had come to the Beach because of, and through, Eric. He was a student in the medical school; Tim was there at the teaching hospital as a resident in orthopedics. He was a fine young doctor, terribly burdened by the care of his young, invalid wife — a girl he had married when he had barely finished med school, and was ready to start his internship. She was to have started teaching in the hospital school for long-term child patients.

They were both very young, and in love, of course. Then, on their honeymoon, less than a week after their marriage, Amy had been hurt. Ever since, she had been an invalid.

"How was she hurt?" asked young Nancy. "Did Tim tell you?"

"No. Just that much. But Eric told us."

"Did he tell Gayle?"

"Oh, heavens, no! She never wants what she calls the gory details."

"I do," said Nancy. "I have liked Tim — I'd like to know."

Later, Mrs. Colburn was to tell that that was the first she had realized Nancy's interest in medicine.

Which was not the reason Nancy had wanted to know as much as she could about Tim Dineen and Amy.

So her mother told what Eric had told the Colburns. That, on the honeymoon, Tim and his bride of three days had gone horseback riding. Amy ahead of Tim. She was a tall, slender girl with auburn hair.

"Was he in love with her?"

"Why, I suppose so, Nancy. They had just been married."

"A'hmmmmn. Go on?"

"Well, it seems that Amy's horse spooked at something, and shied away, reared, so that a branch struck her right across the throat." Mrs. Colburn's pastry wheel gestured. "And it damaged the epiglottis.

157

Caused a swelling. She was unconscious; the swelling cut off oxygen. The brain has to have oxygen. When they got her to the hospital, they did a tracheotomy — opened the throat so she could breath. But Eric said it was too late. She could not talk, walk, or see. She still cannot. It's been over two years. And that poor man . . ."

"Can't they do *anything?*"

"They've tried. The big hospital has tried everything. Eric says one trouble is that this happened to a mature brain. If this happens to a child, he can be trained, slowly to crawl, and perhaps eventually to walk. Glasses and exercises may help the vision. All these things were tried, and are still being tried with Amy, but they are having very little success. She is just beginning to use her right hand. A little. She talks some. But she is terribly depressed most of the time. She has had therapy regularly, but she protests and cries. Lately her heart seems to be weakening. Dr. Dineen says that they should let up, at least for a time. Through Eric, he brought her here. She can be taken out of doors; the air is fresh and clear."

"He's very good to her."

"In so far as he can be."

It was that late summer, seven years ago,

when Nancy began her visits to Amy — as soon as she stopped waiting to see if Gayle was going to become pregnant. She had dreaded that happening. What would any of them have done?

Gayle had not talked to her about her hot session with Tim on the beach. Perhaps because, immediately afterward, the affair seemed to have cooled. Gradually Nancy stopped condemning the man. She realized that he could not divorce Amy and marry Gayle. As she came to know Tim better, she guessed that for a brief interlude, he had stopped thinking of himself as a married man.

But in her mind, Tim still belonged to Gayle. He must have loved her and wanted her. Wouldn't he still want her?

Because Nancy went to see Amy, and did little things for her — when the nurse took her out on the terrace, Nancy sometimes sat beside the wheelchair and talked to Amy, told her about the people, about the ocean; sometimes she read aloud to her. Tim had been grateful. He would talk to the young girl, ask her about the future. By then, Gayle had decided against college, and was working full time in the hotel shop.

She loved doing that sort of thing. Even the women guests enjoyed the way she flirted with all the men who worked for the hotel and with the guests who came there for recreation or business. She couldn't be serious with them all, so probably she was not with any of them. Not as she had been with Tim during that swift time when he had let himself forget Amy and his duty as a husband.

Had Gayle ended that? Probably not. Tim would have been the one, though regretfully, no doubt.

Nancy, fiercely loyal to Dr. Dineen, was sure that he now should and would turn to Gayle. Of course he had said that ridiculous thing yesterday afternoon. Well . . .

Let's see. Where had she got! Yes! To Gayle, and the way she enjoyed her work at the hotel. And the way the guests enjoyed her.

Now Nancy smiled wistfully, recalling the way her pretty sister could cajole almost any man into buying an expensive gift to take home to his wife. She loved that sort of work, she loved the give-and-take gaiety of the resort hotel.

Tim must have seen her. Almost immediately he had set up a routine of regular visits to the Beach. As the years went by, the single room and the nurse which he had originally provided for Amy became a suite where she could be moved about, indoors and out. He affiliated with the Beach Hospital, and came to the hotel each time he had work to do there or consultations to hold. He was doing well in medicine, and by now he was the Chief of Orthopedic Surgery in the big Medical Center, professor in that field at the medical school.

Nancy knew that he worked hard. She had done her own training as a nurse in that hospital; she had specialized directly under Tim's supervision. She knew how hard he worked in the city, here at the Beach Hospital, even on such vacations as he took, generally to seminars or convocations. He was still a young man. Nancy pitied him, she admired him. She really liked him. Certainly he had been kind to *her.*

Of course she knew that he must see Gayle frequently, but it had been rather a shock . . .

Nancy tapped her fingertip against the gray-blue skirt of the dress which had been given to her in jail. Like the canvas shoes, it was too big. This was Sunday. Then it must have been on Friday evening when she had seen Tim with Gayle down on the beach. Still in broad daylight. Gayle had been doing some gymnastics with some man. The sailors had been around. Tim watched

Gayle, and then talked to her.

And Gayle . . . It was hard to know why or how at that distance — Gayle had been able to show her sister that she still loved Tim Dineen. A gesture of her hand, the tip of her head. Had those two been strangers to her, she would have said, "That girl is crazy about that man."

She did seem to be, and this shocked Nancy. Were she and Tim still . . . ?

Six years of growing up had erased some of Nancy's naïveté, but she still remembered that scene at the guard's tower, and kept a lingering belief that such passion, such an embrace, implied *feeling*. Not enduring for Tim, perhaps. Friday night, Gayle had been the one to show urgency and invitation. But, in any case, what about Eric? If Gayle loved Tim, why . . . ?

As a child, Gayle, offered a bowl of bright candies, would always grab a handful, and later, unobserved, would come back to take more. Not because she wanted more candy, but because it was *there*.

Gayle Colburn, while Nancy was busy in the operating rooms, had evidently done what every girl in their neighborhood had attempted. She had set out to catch Eric Ritter, and, in Gayle's case, she had succeeded. She probably did not love him, she probably could not. Especially if she still loved Tim. She still would remember the "affair" she had had with him. If he had been the one to break it off, Gayle would wait, and wait, for the right time and place . . .

Nancy knew about the love which those two had shared. Her parents did not, of course. They would be shocked if Gayle should suddenly turn from Eric to Tim.

They probably were relieved when she had told them that she planned to marry Eric and go to England with him. Her mother had immediately begun to make plans. She had cleaned house, she had made lists and lists and lists. For the wedding, but first for the engagement party. Nancy had come home for her vacation just in time for that.

She wrote something on her tablet. Two week ago, things had been hectic, but all right for her. Normal. She had found herself caught into the vortex of Gayle's party, with no time to be sorry for Eric, no time to think if something couldn't be done to prevent the marriage. Gayle would not make a good wife for any kind and gentle man. She needed a shouter and a beater.

The wedding might never take place, though there were plans for that, too. Just the families at the church because of Grandma's death, and afterward a reception for friends in Dad's rose garden.

"They'll ruin your flowers," Nancy had warned him.

"I know it, dear. I am glad roses have thorns, the bushes will survive."

But first must come the engagement party, though Nancy was not sure why it had to come at all.

If she had been looking back at the party from any other place and position in her life, Nancy even now could have laughed about the way her mother's plans and Gayle's ideas had clashed and sent sparks all over the place.

Tea cakes and dainty sandwiches, said her mother. A tart, refreshing punch with white grapes frozen into a green ring to serve as ice in the silver bowl.

Champagne punch, Gayle amended. And some snappy hot canapés in addition to the ribbon sandwiches and the tiny ham biscuits.

They clashed on every point. Even where a chair should be placed, and certainly on whether extra folding chairs should be available.

Roses and daisies would indeed make a pretty centerpiece, but wouldn't her mother even *try* a mound of white grapes simply heaps of them — with a yellow rosebud tucked in here and there? And silver candlesticks. She could borrow some tall ones from the hotel . . .

Tears were shed and compromises were reached. Some champagne was added to their mother's punch. Nancy was delegated to heat the fancy canapés — and fell down on the job. Chairs were set out for their mother's friends, and some of Gayle's sank gratefully into them when they came to the party at the end of a warm day. There were no grapes on the tea table, but there were no daisies or hotel candlesticks, either.

But, all in all, it was a lovely party. And it was Gayle's party. "She's a genius at making people have a good time," Nancy told her mother.

"Yes, she is, Nancy. We have the bruises to prove that!"

"We'll have all this stuff to put away, won't we?"

"Yes, of course. And we must do it. Eric and Gayle have gone off somewhere."

Nancy was gathering the crumpled little napkins. "Can you do these in the washer?" she asked.

"Put them in the nylon sack. But, yes, they will launder. They are linen."

"All nine hundred and eight of them. Mom . . . ?"

"Yes, dear?" Her mother was sorting out the dishes and crystal, ready to wash them.

"Do you think this is going to work?"

"I don't put my Haviland or cut glass into the washer, dear."

Nancy laughed. "I didn't men the *dishes!* I was talking about Gayle's marrying Eric. Do you think that is going to work?"

"Now, Nancy . . ."

"I know. He seems to be crazy about her. But —"

"But you're still remembering the crush you had on him ten years ago." Her mother's face was kind.

"Not *ten,* Mom! When I was thirteen, I hated boys."

"Yes, you did. Though Gayle, at thirteen . . ."

"I remember. Boys hung around. Maybe that's why I didn't like them. They didn't hang around me."

"Enough of them did, when you were old enough. You've always had beaus, Nancy. Don't you, in the city?"

"They're not called beaus, but, yes, I have dates. Nothing serious, of course."

"I hoped you had got over your crush on Eric."

"Why should I even try? He's always lovely to me, but there's never been any sign that he returned my passion for him."

"My dear . . ."

"I'm sorry, Mom. But believe me, when I asked you if you thought this engagement would work, I was not being jealous. I was wondering if Gayle was ready and willing to be a doctor's wife."

She listened to, she heard, her mother's arguments pro and con that situation. It seemed that the Colburns had worried about the matter.

And as she talked, Nancy had examined her feeling for Eric. She was not at all sure that she had indeed got over her "crush." Nearly always when she saw him, she felt that she still had it. She did like the big, blond man; she liked everything about him, and if something dizzy and delightful could come of that liking, she would be the happiest girl in the world!

Her mother, by then, was saying some things about not ever trying to freeze black walnuts again. And then she went on to say that, even today, when Gayle's engagement to Eric was being announced, she had overheard some of the women say that they would not have been surprised to have Gayle take out after — "That was their phrase, Nancy! It really was. They would not have been surprised to see Gayle take out after Grampa."

Nancy gasped.

"They called him 'that old man,' but they meant Grampa, of course."

Nancy was stunned. "They even," said her mother, "decided that she still might do it. Then they went on to say that she had been lovely to him ever since Grandma died."

"Well, I've always been lovely to him," said Nancy indignantly, "and nobody thinks . . ."

"Because you *always* have been lovely to him, dear. But Gayle . . . Oh, of course, there's always this sort of talk when a rich man becomes a widower."

But even if Gayle, recently, had become "lovely" to Mr. Ritter —

"It's a ridiculous idea!" cried Nancy. "Why, Frances Parmeley would interfere if Eric didn't!" She vigorously polished a cut glass cup. "And Grampa himself — He's old, but he isn't foolish. He dearly loved Grandma."

Her mother made no comment.

"But Frances is the one who would take care of that situation!" said Nancy firmly. "Did she come to the party?"

"No. She sent her regrets. She isn't well, Nancy. She may not even know of the speculation about her father."

"The whole family is living at the hotel."

"Yes, they are. Since Mrs. Ritter became ill last winter. But Frances — several months ago — Frances had some sort of surgery. I heard it was a small brain tumor removed . . ."

Nancy clashed silver forks and spoons into a pan. "Might as well wash them all," she grumbled. "You know what, Mom? I'm *sick* of people with brain injuries!"

Mrs. Colburn turned in shocked surprise. "Why, Nancy . . ."

"I know, I know. This Florence Nightingale is supposed to *glow* at the sight of blood! What do we do with all these fancy canapés that didn't get eaten?"

"I'll check them. Some will freeze. And maybe I'm wrong about Frances. The surgery she had. I do know she has not been well. Did you notice Barbara this afternoon?"

"Well, of course I noticed her. Speaking of crushes, she really has one on Gayle."

"Yes, she does. I've tried to talk to Gayle about her responsibilities in that situation."

"Did she listen?"

"I hope so."

Barbara, the oldest Parmeley child, a girl of sixteen, had shadowed Gayle all afternoon, scarcely taking her eyes from the honoree at the party. Barbara was lovely in her own right. Perhaps Nancy could say a word or two to Eric. "Doesn't Barbara go to the College?" she asked. In this family, that meant Dr. Colburn's school.

"Yes, she does. But there again, her mother's illness seems to have had an unfortunate influence. She's at an impressionable age."

"Who isn't?" asked Nancy, busily sorting silver. And more busily, in her mind, going back over the long afternoon. Barbara, a slim, dark-haired shadow of Gayle who had simply sparkled! Her dress had been perfect. White linen, and simple. Simply perfect.

"Of course it came from the boutique!" one of the guests had said.

"She never shows me dresses like that!" complained another.

"Go around tomorrow. It will be back in stock."

Nancy, circulating with her trays, had soon become part of the unnoticed background. Even as she offered cheese puffs and smoked salmon, one of Gayle's friends could ask another why she supposed Gayle finally was settling on Eric. "Busy little bee that she is, there still must be ones . . ."

"But she seems to want to be married, darling. To have the independence of a married woman." The speaker drank from her glass cup. "And of course she's marrying Ritter because of all that lovely money!"

The woman spoke flippantly, and no one who heard seemed to take them seriously. Except Nancy. She had had a sinking feeling of the cats' claws having exposed too much of the truth. If Eric knew — But of course he must know that his family's wealth had always featured in his life. Except in his work as a surgical resident, it had made many differences. Certainly with girls it had.

Not girls like Nancy. He passed her off as a sweet kid.

Did he think Gayle was like her sister? Oh, he couldn't! Eric was a smart guy. He must know they were not one bit alike.

As the gay party progressed, as Gayle's friends replaced the more discreet, the more kind older women, Gayle became the direct target of some barbed raillery. She appeared to enjoy the attack, and answered brashly in kind. When someone asked what she meant to do about all her past loves, Gayle pretended to list them.

"The poor dears," she called them. "Let

me see. There was that basketball player in high school — or did he play football? And there was the young curate at our church." There certainly had been! "And the maitre d' of the Palm Court at the hotel . . ."

"What about that doctor?" asked some young woman shrilly.

Gayle's face went bland. "Eric's a doctor," she said innocently. Nancy felt her face getting hot.

"Don't try that on me, Gayle Colburn! You know I'm talking about the doctor who comes to the hotel to see his wife, and walks with you along the beach late at night."

"Oh, that doctor," drawled Gayle, trying to sound indifferent.

"You bet, that doctor! Wasn't that a pretty hot thing you had with him!"

"She was being sorry for him," drawled another voice.

Gayle laughed brightly. "Are you talking about *Tim?*" she asked. "Of course I was sorry for Tim. I still am! And it's still hot between us. I mean to keep it that way, too. Yes, I really do. I am serving notice. With Eric a busy, genius doctor, I'll have to have *someone!*"

This was met with small screams of laughter and protest. Nancy took her half-full tray back to the kitchen and waited there for the guests to leave.

Gayle making up a story bothered her, but Gayle speaking the truth scared her half to death.

Chapter 8

It was not that same evening — but the next, or maybe even the second one after, that Eric came down along the beach to where Nancy was scraping paint from her father's small boat. She had spread a tarp on the clean sand, and kept the project up among a clump of weathered dwarf pines. She also had asked permission from Grampa. "It's almost at the end of the hotel beach," she said.

"You go right ahead, sweetheart," Grampa had told her. "I myself would rather you'd be on our beach. I don't want any ruffian bothering you."

Grampa talked that way.

She had worked all day, bringing her lunch from home, and once going into the water for a swim. People had spoken to her, but generally she was alone. The arc of clean sand, the bordering half-circle of the hotel buildings, and the people on its terraces, the houses of the town beyond that, and, in the other direction, the ocean, its waves low, lazy under an almost dead calm wind — this was what she had come home to get. Peace,

174

warm sun, a chance to think, or better yet, no need to think at all.

She scraped, and kept the paint chips neatly into heaps on the tarpaulin. She talked to those who talked to her, and went on doing what she was doing. Yes, she would paint the bottom. Oh, of course she was good at it. No, she didn't live around here, she just came down to scrape the boat. Yes, she could sail it. Yes, it did have a small inboard.

And all the time she had her own thoughts going through her head like ducks in a carnival shooting gallery. She thought about the big hospital complex, and her work in the surgical suites. This brought Tim Dineen into line. So she thought about the big doctor. And then she thought about Amy. It seemed to Nancy that Amy was going downhill. For a while she had progressed, but for the last two times she had seen Tim's wife she could detect no improvement. Poor Tim.

And then she thought about Gayle. And the engagement party. And the upcoming wedding where Nancy was supposed to be bridesmaid in white swiss embroidered muslin over pale green, a floppy brimmed hat with green velvet ribbons, and —

By then, Nancy should be, would be back

in the city. And she hoped she could honestly say that her duties at the hospital would not permit her to be a bridesmaid at Gayle's wedding. At Eric's.

Having reached this point, not for the first time that day, she only gulped when she heard Eric's shout, and, turning her head, could see him slogging through some drifted sand to join her. The rising breeze tossed his hair about his head. White-capped waves were kicking up in the water beyond.

"Oh, I'm glad you're out here, Nancy!" he cried, finding a place to sit beside her.

"I set it up," she assured him.

"Bait, huh?"

"Of course."

"Is this why you came home? Or does your dad make you earn board and bed?"

"Ever since I was twenty-one."

He laughed and stretched his arms. "I should be studying," he told her.

"You don't need to cram."

"I sure want to pass those Boards."

"You will, won't you?"

"Oh, I'll *pass* them, but I want to make diplomate, and get that job in England."

"What sort of job is it, Eric?"

"Haven't I told you?"

"I hardly see you. I didn't even know you

were planning to be married until I came home."

Now, ten days later, it was like a movie to the Nancy who wore a gray-blue prison smock and sat on a hard stool in the cement-block cell. The beach, the ocean, the man in his blue slacks and white shirt, his blowing yellow hair. Yes, and that other Nancy in white ducks and a striped tank shirt, catching her own blowing hair and tying it with a twisted scarf. Even the talk — it was like dialogue heard in a play, between two pictured people. They spoke of England, though England did not really exist. Not in the sense that the sand and the ocean and the hotel behind them existed. Eric said he would continue the research in spinal ganglia which he had already begun. But he would "practice." He would do surgery.

"And be called Mister, not Doctor."

"That, too," he agreed.

"But you'll be a specialist, not a resident."

"I'll be a 'consultant.' In surgery. I go along with the use and development of some new sophisticated equipment and techniques."

"A junior consultant? I've heard that term, or read it in some English book."

"I'll be a *senior* consultant, or specialist.

What I've been doing here is junior consultant work."

Nancy pressed her hands to her brow. "It sounds very complicated and exciting, too, of course. And you'll live in London. I do envy Gayle."

"Your time will come," he promised her. Kindly, speaking as a grown man to a child of whom he was fond.

For a couple of years this manner had been irritating Nancy, coming from Eric. And, not for the first time, she reminded him of the work she did at the Medical Center.

He had laughed at her, and said he *knew* she was the best of all surgical technicians. "Maybe I'll get you to come to London and work with me."

"Gayle would really love that!" she retorted.

Laughing, he had hugged her. And then gone right on talking about medicine, getting enthusiastic about the research which he planned to do.

She'd teased him and called him a chiropractor, with his ideas that so many human ills could be traced to the spine.

He'd thumped her for that and suggested that she was neglecting her paint scraping. "And I should be getting back to my books," he'd added, not moving.

"I can't make any of these things come true," he told her, "unless I pass these blasted Boards."

"Are you worried, really, Eric?" she had asked.

"I really am, Nancy. I feel that this is my big chance. And those orals loom ahead of me like the face of a high cliff. These people want a diplomate, and just passing won't give me that."

"They won't find a better candidate than you are."

"Maybe not. But I want to be *me*. This is my chance to get myself clear out from under the burden which the family name and money puts upon me. To be my own man and do my own work."

And Gayle was marrying him for that very name and that money. Nancy had stared at the man, feeling an impulse to urge him to free himself of Gayle, too. Did he think, in London, she would be willing to live on a "senior consultant's" income, to share only the glory of his medical achievements? Oh, she should rescue Eric! He wouldn't love Nancy, but he might be able . . . Her busy mind began to spin wheels and hunt for ways and means.

By then Eric was talking about Tim, and

Nancy wondered if that freedom could be accomplished through Tim. If Dr. Dineen still loved Gayle, he might have his own reasons for breaking up this marriage before it happened. Just maybe . . .

For ten minutes Eric had been talking about what Tim had done for him. "He came down last weekend and gave me several hours of briefing on what I'll meet in the orals. I couldn't *have* better coaching!"

"He's a great guy in many ways," Nancy said earnestly. "Maybe I know that better than you do."

"It's possible. Though I have worked with him, some. But do you know what I think was the greatest thing he ever did?" He didn't wait for Nancy to answer. He told her.

"It was after that big accident up the coast highway," he said, hugging his knees and gazing out before him. "Remember? Last August, I think it was. One of the victims was a woman whose leg was severed. The radio reported that a surgeon at the Medical Center was attempting to restore the leg after the state police recovered it and rushed it to the hospital 'minutes after the accident.' I remember exactly the words used. I had already figured the surgeon must be Dineen.

"And I was positive when this 'surgeon,' who never was named, came on the horn to say that no attempt ever had been made to restore the leg because that was not medically feasible. He had made the decision because the wound was a jagged one with a high degree of contamination. He said, 'We never really entertained any idea of reimplanting. The cases that had been successfully done were relatively clean amputations.' "

"I remember that night," said Nancy soberly. "Tim was upset by the news stories."

"Did you work in that o.r.?"

"I did. But Tim still didn't tell the whole story. The 'minutes' in which the severed limb was delivered was also incorrect. The thing was first taken ten miles in the opposite direction from where the woman was."

Eric laughed and shrugged. "That figures. Did she recover?"

"Of course. I believe she has been fitted with an artificial leg and is using it."

"I said it was his greatest job. In overall performance and one hundred per cent honesty."

Even as they talked about it, Nancy thought of that "greatest job." Multiple injury accidents were always bad for the orthopedic surgery department. This had happened on a rainy night, extra crews were called in from their families, dates, and special occasions. She could remember the way Dr. Dineen had looked. Because it was the way he always looked. Big, calm, pleasant to those around him. His dark eyes alert, his hands gentle and skillful.

She said some of these things to Eric.

"You love the man, don't you?" he asked her.

This startled her. "I admire him," she conceded. "I know him like a member of the family. He's been very good to me, Eric."

"I know he has. Great guns, girl, I admire him tremendously myself!"

They spent that pleasant hour together, though at the end of it Nancy could not see the slightest sign that Eric would ever look on her as anything but Gayle's little sister. She had watched him closely, and now could remember each detail. How he held his hand, his fingers. How his jaw would knot when he was earnest about something, how his whole face brightened when he smiled . . .

He thought of Nancy as young, which she was. But to her he also seemed young to be planning on marriage. And she did mention twice that he was young in years and medical experience to be taking the prestigious

Board examinations.

As he argued his side of that decision, she, knowing his position, scraped paint and wondered if there was anything she could do or say to him about his present situation, which she considered a "mess." Meaning his plans to marry Gayle, and hers to marry him when she was still in love with Tim and had said that she meant to hold onto him. Could Nancy do *anything?*

She could try — and she did try, bungling and blundering, of course.

She tried for the light approach; she told Eric, as being a joke, what some of Gayle's friends had teased her about at the engagement party. "They kept dragging Tim's name into it. In Gayle's place I would have resented that. I know she used to be very fond of Tim, but if she is marrying you, that should be over, and her friends should know it, don't you think?"

To that, Eric, with his jaw knotted, had only made patterns in the sand with a stick.

But when she went on — Oh, now Nancy could not recall her exact words — though perhaps she did not want to remember them. Something about Eric's being sure Gayle was over it. He was, wasn't he? And Eric had slapped her ears down. He really did. She was still hurt by his attack. And puzzled. Did he really think he could trust Gayle? Implicitly?

That was one of the things he had said. "I trust Gayle implicitly."

Hooo boy!

But she had not said *that!*

She thought he might walk out on her for saying such a "silly" thing about Gayle, but evidently he was still regarding her as Gayle's foolish young sister. Because after a pause, during which she worked and he stared at a boat out in the water, he asked her if she knew his cousin Barbara Parmeley.

Nancy glanced at him, nodding. "Yes! Of course I've *known* her for some time."

"I suppose you have. But now they — the family — are living at the hotel."

"I know. She's growing up fast."

"Yes, she is. And she has developed a heavy crush on Gayle."

Which Nancy had observed at the party. Barbara had frequently come to the house since.

"She tries to talk like Gayle," said Eric, smiling. "She copies her clothes, and her mannerisms . . . I get a kick out of it."

"A lot of girls get these crushes. At her age, especially." Nancy had wanted to add that since he was so enthralled with Gayle, he must think this crush a fine thing! She didn't say it. She wasn't going to say another word about Gayle to Eric Ritter. If he was smart enough to take and pass the Board exams, he should know Gayle for himself. And, for another thing, maybe Nancy *was* jealous of her sister! Yep! Darned right, she was! She began again to listen to what Eric was saying.

Something about the family's having worried some about Barbara. And then he went on to say that he hoped Gayle — because of the crush, Nancy knew? — he hoped that Gayle could do something about Barbara, and for her. Did Nancy think he should point out this opportunity to Gayle?

"Well," said Nancy, taking off her glove and brushing her hair out of her face, "I suppose it would help Gayle. I know it would help me to know just why Barbara needs advice or assistance. She seems quite sure of herself . . ."

Eric nodded. "I have a way of backing into things," he admitted. "Yes, Barbara is very poised and sure that she knows what she is doing. But she is only sixteen, and last fall it seems that she fell in love with a boy whom she met away at school."

"She goes to our college here, doesn't she?"

"Now, she does. But then she went to another one. In Ohio. After Grandma died and the family moved here — partly because of this boy and her love affair, too — Uncle Eugene had her transferred here."

"I see," said Nancy, wondering where Gayle came in.

"Of course Barbara wasn't happy about that, but the family had to stay on here. Aunt Francey became ill . . ."

"Brain tumor," Nancy murmured.

Eric glanced at her. "You knew about all this?"

"Oh, no. Just that Mrs. Parmeley had had brain surgery."

Eric relaxed. "Yes, she did. She is getting along all right, but these things take time. And Barbara should not be a worry to her."

"But she is."

"I don't suppose she thinks that she is, though I've tried to explain to her. And I don't believe I've helped much. I do think Gayle would have more luck."

"Why don't you ask her?"

"Would it be as simple as that? I don't want her to think I stand ready to plunge her into a lot of family problems."

Along with the family money, what could make Gayle happier? thought Nancy. Even now she did not blush at the thought.

"I think she could help," Eric mused. "You see, Barbara insists she is going to marry this fellow, and do it this summer, willy-nilly! At sixteen, that seems terrible to all of us. If I thought Gayle could help . . ."

"I expect she'd love to try. Maybe some sound advice would cure Barbara of her crush, and if she gave that advice to the guy, he could maybe fall in love with Gayle instead. Most of you young fellows do."

Eric gave her a shove that tumbled her into the scrub pine. "You're certainly hard on your sister," he told her, pulling her out again.

Nancy examined her scratches. "Those things are pin cushions!" she told the young man.

"I'm sorry."

"You are not. And I don't know what you mean by my being hard on Gayle. No one is hard on her."

"Nancy . . ."

"If I'd say to her what I just said to you, that most of you young fellows fall for her, she'd be pleased. She really would. It's always happened. Since she was twelve, and it keeps on happening. You fell for her, Tim Dineen did." She brushed her paint flakes into a heap. "I just wish," she said ruefully, "that it would happen to me."

"Aw, now, Nancy, we all love you!"

"Sure you do. Good old Nancy. Which is not the way you feel about Gayle."

"Are you really jealous?"

She thought about that. "Not really," she admitted. "I wouldn't want to be and do many of the things that come naturally to her. For instance, I wouldn't talk to my mother the way Gayle does when she wants her own way about something. You know how she is, Eric. She *must* have her way!"

"Oh, yes," he agreed. "And she usually gets it. Don't you get yours?"

"Not in the same way. If I think I'm right, I keep trying, but — well, you know me, and you know Gayle. We are not much alike."

He contemplated this fact. "Have *you* any suggestions about Barbara?" he asked.

"Do you know this boy? Maybe he'd be all right . . ."

"Sixteen is too young to get married."

Nancy smiled. "A lot of girls do."

"Because they have to."

"Not always, but — well, my only suggestion is what I said before. Invite the boy here. How old is he, by the way?"

"He's twenty."

"An older man, huh?"

"He's a sophomore at some college. Barbara went to a junior school, and met him at dances or things."

"I get the picture. And from her point of view he would be an older man."

"All right. We invite him here. What do we do then?"

"Be nice to him. Very nice. And before he leaves have a talk with him. Say that you understand their wish to be married, but wouldn't it be better — the family thinks it would be better — if he would go back and finish school, that he would be welcome to visit Barbara, but she, too, should finish school."

"I get the picture. Do you think it would work, Nancy?"

She shrugged. "I think it could work, Eric. If he's the right sort of guy. Maybe his own family wants him to do just that. Though perhaps the Ritter money is dazzling them away from good sense."

"Oh, now, look!" Eric protested. "I don't think that needs bringing up."

"Doesn't it? I mean, doesn't it dazzle everyone?"

"I wouldn't know," he said stiffly.

"Maybe," Nancy had persisted, more than half seriously, "Maybe it's why I am so very fond of you. Maybe it's why Gayle is, too."

He snorted. "The money doesn't matter with you two."

Nancy shrugged again, and began to gather her tools.

"You said that all men fall in love with Gayle. But I'm the one she says she'll marry. There's a big difference."

Nancy stood up. "And I hope that will work out, too, Eric. I hope you pass your Boards, and I hope you do good work in England."

"With Gayle," he added.

She was busy folding the tarp. Suddenly she felt tired. There was no use talking to Eric, no use hoping that he would listen to what she said. All the men were blind to what Gayle was. Eric was one of them. To his question, she said she might, or might not, paint the boat the next day. "I may cut my vacation short," she said, sure that her disappointment showed in her voice. "I may just go back to work."

She was disappointed. She walked up the sand beside him, and then went home.

Now, in her cell, she wondered if Eric knew, or cared, that she was being held for questioning about Amy's death. Wouldn't he come to see her if he did know? He probably knew better — He'd *said* that he thought Amy had committed suicide.

Chapter 9

After what must have been at least an hour of comparative quiet in the jail . . .

Was this what the newspaper called the holdover? Nancy wondered idly, then realizing where her thoughts had strayed, and on top of *that* realizing where she *was,* panic once more began to lay its hold upon her. She saw this in the tremor of her hand as she held the pencil and tried to doodle on the pad of white paper. She felt the flush of it on her cheeks, and in the quickening of her pulse. She stood up and walked about. She must quit this! Nothing had changed. Nothing in her thinking convinced her that she was anything but Ann Justine Colburn, called Nancy, surgical technician, registered and practicing. A nice girl with good manners and ill will to no one.

She gulped, making a funny sound, and she walked to the bars of the gate, or door, and tried to see what the confusion was down the hall. A policewoman, matron, or whatever she was called, came down the hall and Nancy asked her.

"Just a drunk," said the woman. "We get them on Sunday mornings. This fellow — he comes in regularly. A real alcoholic."

"Then he's sick."

"I guess," said the woman, going on.

Nancy shrugged, and sat down again to reread the notes which she had made. Should she go on? Examine the remaining ten days which led up to last night, and this morning, and . . .

She might as well. Not much of anything seemed about to happen here and now. Except maybe lunch. And she certainly could wait for that!

Let's see. She had scraped the boat and talked to Eric, and decided to go back to the city, though of course she did not go. The next day Eric had gone off to take his Board exams, and Nancy had finished the paint scraping, then got ready to put on new paint. She liked doing that; she always had been neat and skillful with her hands. She could print, and draw nicely. The ability was a big help in the work she did in the operating rooms. With needle, scissors, or even a scalpel, she could move quickly and exactly. This made things easier for the patient. And helped the surgeons, they said.

Resting her chin on her hand, her thoughts went back again to the hospital, to the operating rooms, to Dr. Dineen.

The day she finished the boat painting, she had cleaned up and taken a handful of roses to Amy. Perfumed roses, and pretty ones. She had guided Amy's hand to touch the soft, cool petals and had described them to the blind woman. She didn't even know if these services reached Amy, who could talk but did very little of it.

And it was that same evening — late in the afternoon — that she had met Tim, in of all places, the supermarket. She had driven her mother's car there, with a list.

Across the low display counters of beautifully arranged vegetables and fruits, Tim had called to her. Now, where she was, Nancy could close her eyes and see the colors, all the shades of green, the bright reds, and oranges — lettuce, tomatoes, bananas — bronzed pears and earthy mushrooms, great bright strawberries . . .

"Wait till I get around there," he had said. Nancy had slowed her own progress, watching his tall, dark head, wondering what on earth he was doing in the supermarket.

When he came down the aisle toward her, she asked him.

He laughed and gestured to the assortment in his cart. "I came to the Beach for a little job and to ask Ritter about the Board exams," he explained. "He won't get in until six, so I'm getting my week's shopping done. I planned to drop by your house long enough to thank you for the flowers you brought Amy."

She flipped her hand. "Dad raises 'em. I just pick 'em and bring 'em."

"You pick ones that smell sweet —"

"Well . . ."

"That's thoughtfulness, Nancy. Flowers for a blind person should have perfume."

"It must be terrible, Tim —"

"I imagine it is terrible. And ten years of it, Nancy! Does she ever complain to you?"

"Oh, no. Lately, she cries sometimes. She never has talked much."

"I know. I sit and talk to her, hoping she understands."

"I do the same thing. I call it *babbling*."

"Well, I do thank you. It must help. I can't tell, can you? If she seems more depressed lately? She has been depressed, of course, since the first. But lately she won't show interest in anything." He moved his cart out of someone's way.

Nancy pointed to the things which he had selected. Bread, fruit — soap powder — napkins —

"Are you about to set up housekeeping?" she asked.

He looked surprised. "Glory be, girl!" he cried. "I am already set up! and have been for five years or more."

"In a *house?*" She had supposed he lived in a hotel, or someplace . . .

"Well, it's an apartment," he amended. "One bedroom, living room, bath and kitchen. Sure I keep house. You didn't think I maintained my figure on hospital food?"

She giggled.

"I cook," he bragged. "Clean — wash my socks and undies — the works. Come up and see me sometime."

She laughed aloud. "I may do that!" she threatened.

He patted her arm and gestured toward the deli behind the bakery counter. "Let's get a cup of coffee or some iced tea."

"Okay. And you can tell me how you avoid dishpan hands."

"Oh, that's easy. I have a dishwasher, or I use paper plates."

Laughing, they sat down at a small table and ordered iced tea. "Seriously," said Tim, "I'd like to have you see my place. I furnished it. Ready-furnished places cost too much. You know, dear, my chief extravagance is Amy."

Nancy nodded. "I know it must cost a mint."

"It does. The costs hit me pretty hard when she was first hurt. And me an intern. I went into debt . . ."

"Her family . . ."

"She has a sister, married, with four kids. Her mother died two years after we were — married."

Nancy wondered if he still felt married. And if he did, how he could . . . She squeezed the slice of lemon into her tea.

"I've been thinking," she said slowly, "that I might cut my vacation."

"Aren't you having a good time?"

She shrugged. "I love the beach and swimming — but — Oh, I don't know. I painted Dad's little boat . . . But that's finished."

"I thought you came here for the wedding."

"I didn't know until I got here that there was to be a wedding."

"It's to be soon, isn't it?"

"It had better be," she said brightly, "or Gayle will change her mind. Maybe even Eric might." Then she went on to tell Tim some of the things she had said, or tried to say, to Eric on the beach a couple of days before. He watched her and listened. With his doctor's face and attention. A doctor's eyes. Interested, concerned, not showing what *he* was thinking.

"I wonder," she concluded, "if you couldn't think of the right thing to do or say."

"To Eric?" he asked. "What could I say? He knows he's rich, and swims through waters full of baited hooks."

"I meant, say something to Gayle. She'd listen to you."

"I don't think so, Nancy."

"She would if you'd say the right things. You could make her see what she may be doing to a rising young doctor."

Tim shook his head. "No way," he said firmly. "I plan to keep my hands off, in all directions. And I'll add this, young lady. You had better do the same thing. You'd be happier."

"But —"

"Maybe this marriage isn't right. Maybe it won't last. But anything I might say won't change things, my dear. Gayle is Gayle, and it would be impossible to change that. Or her."

He was right, of course. But Nancy was disappointed. There had been a time, she was sure, when a word from Tim would have changed Gayle. "I thought . . ." she began, then went on to say what she had in mind. "I thought you liked Gayle."

Tim laughed freely, happily. "No one, my darling Nancy," he said earnestly, "no *man* — *likes* a girl like Gayle. I can't imagine where your Mom and Dad found her. There is excitement where she is concerned. There is *passion*. But liking? The idea itself is ridiculous."

Nancy's chin lifted. "Are you suggesting that I should be sorry for her?" she asked. "To me, *that* idea is ridiculous."

He reached for her hand and briefly held it warmly in his own. Now, after a week, Nancy could still feel his touch. "Sometime," he said quietly, "sometime you probably will be sorry for her, Nancy."

That was all that was said then. But Nancy went home in a dream. This business of *liking*, she thought. Of one thing she was certain. She *liked* Tim Dineen.

She liked him now, at this minute, in this cold and bare jail cell. She would tell him so the next time she saw him. Which would be soon, because he knew she had not killed Amy, and would do things about it.

She would tell him she liked him, and probably make a new kind of fool of herself. Just as yesterday she had sounded and been foolish when she told him to marry Gayle;

he'd said what he had about passion and excitement to tell her that he didn't love Gayle. And, for all of her stupidity, he had said . . .

She gazed up at the window and thought about what he had said. And for half an hour, her dreams were able to take her away from the city jail, away from the Beach . . .

It was a rude awakening to realize that people, passing along the corridor, would stop and look in at her through the square grid in the door. She could see only their heads, their eyes . . . But it was terrible to be stared at so, not to be able to shield herself . . . not to know, even, who those people were! She turned her back, and, finally, she moved the stool to a position against the door, and sat there, feeling triumphant. Now, the best anyone could see would be the top of her head, maybe her feet extended before her. Her feet in those awful, loose, canvas shoes.

So seated, she picked up her little tablet and pencil and tried to remember just what had happened next in the progress of her vacation. The rest of that first week had passed, she'd swum, she'd seen some of her friends, she had shopped with her mother. Eric had gone off to St. Louis to take the exams, and had returned, looking drawn and nervous. "I'm sure I failed," he told Nancy when he passed her in the hotel lobby.

That lobby. Big, beautiful, bright colors, flowers, soft music, thronging people, most of them having a good time. Bellhops and managers walking double time, groups of people in bright resort clothes laughing and talking happily. Dogs being taken out, or brought in — the page going — pictures being taken of a minor celebrity.

Grampa in his tall-backed chair, watching it all, quick to detect the least variance in what was normal confusion. A slight gesture of his hand could give important directions. Would Eugene Parmeley, or anyone, ever be able to manage things the way Grampa did, even now, when age and grief had laid a heavy hand upon him?

And then, in the middle of the second week — Nancy could not really say if it was Wednesday or Thursday — she rather thought Wednesday, because so much happened after it — but anyway, in midweek, word came . . .

Eric was in o.r. when the radio told the news as an event of great local interest. He had a crisis to handle. During his absence a G.P. had tied off a patient's femoral artery;

after he had performed a varicose vein ligation, his patient had suffered intense leg pains. Without examining the leg, the doctor had prescribed quinine. Now the woman had been brought to the Beach Hospital, and Dr. Ritter examined her. In panic, he put in a call to the Medical Center for Dr. Dineen, who was in surgery. Then Eric decided that he should know what had happened, and what he should do.

The woman's leg was gray-blue from mid-thigh down. He was sure that the so-called surgeon had tied the femoral artery near the groin, so the leg had gone four days without circulation.

Dr. Ritter and the second-year surgical resident cut out a section of the artery, sewed the ends together. Eric ordered the anesthetist to do a splanchnic block, hoping to restore circulation again, but right there on the table, the leg turned pink to the ankle, but the foot remained gray, and amputation would surely have to be done. Eric turned from the table and asked all within hearing what jackass could not tell the saphenous vein from the femoral artery? "I know I don't want any more referrals from *him!*"

And it was at this point of anger and frustration that the word came to him. To those who worked with him. To the hospital.

It came to the hotel, to Grampa, who shrugged, and to Gayle in the boutique, who was arranging a spread of long gold chains in the lobby display window. She heard the news, she repeated it to herself, and then she stepped back into the shop, between the headless figure which displayed an orange-edged black bikini on its gleaming silver torso and the brass rack of floating long scarfs. And her angry comment should have shriveled the pearl-set chain she still held in her hands. She tossed it, rattling, on the counter and stalked out of the shop.

The word came to Nancy. Her mother brought it to her, meeting her halfway down the path between the rose beds. "Have you had the radio on, dear?" she asked.

Nancy spread out her hands. Bathing suit — red checkered with perky ruffles of white embroidery — red canvas sneakers. Her terry beach robe, but no beach bag or radio.

So her mother told her, and Nancy stood rubbing her bare arms, which had turned cold and numb.

Eric had not passed the Board exams. Well, yes, he had passed them, but not well enough to be given diplomate classification which he had wanted. He could specialize, she explained to her anxious mother, but he would not be given anything more than a certificate of specialization. He had not been given a diplomate.

She tried to explain further. A diplomate was something like a Ph.D., she said. It marked the heights of study and achievement. It — She shivered.

"Does this mean," asked her mother, "that he won't get the big job he had counted on?"

"If that was a specification, I suppose it means just that! Oh, poor Eric!"

"The news said he will now be on the staff of the Beach Hospital," her mother offered hopefully.

"He's a very good doctor," Nancy assured her. "Very good!"

"I am sure he is, dear. I'm sure we all think so."

All but Eric, thought Nancy, going in to shower and dress. She would see Eric, give him a chance to talk about it. And maybe Tim would come down. Should she send word to him?

She considered going directly to the hospital and asking to see Eric. This idea she quickly discarded, but she would watch for him to return to his home, the hotel. If she could talk to him! She both understood and sympathized with his disappointment.

More than anyone else could, she thought.

So she dressed and went to the hotel, haunting the veranda and the halls nearest the hospital. She might miss him . . . But she did not.

People passed her. A man in a striped red and white jacket over red swim trunks, a slick-haired girl with him. A lifeguard taking a break, a navy blue warm-up pulled on above his figured trunks, his long hair blowing in the breeze. He stopped to talk to Nancy, even offered to buy her lunch.

No . . . She was waiting for someone. But she smiled at the guard, and thanked him. Her gaze swept the beach, then returned to the road and walk that led from the hospital. Eric would come. He'd not want to listen to what the hospital folk would have to say. He might not even want to listen to Nancy . . .

But she waited. And, after more than an hour, she saw him — white shirt, white duck trousers, but with his jacket left behind, the sun shining on his hair. He walked fast. Nancy moved toward him. Even from a distance, his face showed how sunk he was, how disappointed and discouraged.

As he would have passed her, he looked up. "Oh, hello, Nancy," he said dispiritedly.

She put out her hand. "Eric . . ."

"You've heard, haven't you?"

"Yes. I wish there were something I could do or say."

He tried to smile. "Me, too," he said.

"I am terribly sorry, Eric."

"I know you are." They stepped up into the shadow of the walkway.

"You did pass, you know."

"Not with any distinction. And for me, that isn't good enough."

"Why, it is too, Eric Ritter! For a man your age. You can do the research you planned. You must work hard at that, and have the results to back you up when you try the Boards again."

He stopped where he was. Beyond the arches of this passage, the flowering trees blew in the wind, now in sunshine, now in shade. He took Nancy's two elbows in his hands. He bent and kissed her. "You know?" he said. "I really do love you, Nancy."

She was flustered, she blushed, she stammered. "Oh, shucks!" she cried. "If that is so, why did you go and get yourself engaged to Gayle?"

He drew a deep breath and looked out over her head to the distant view of white sand and blue water. "That's a question I often ask myself," he said gravely. And without another word, he went quickly through a door and into the hotel.

Nancy stood where she was. She supposed Eric would seek Gayle.

And what would Gayle find to say to him? Would she know the right attitude to take with him?

Nancy strolled down toward the beach; she met and spoke to — answered — a couple of people. Yes, it was a gorgeous day. A specialty of Peter's Beach. Yes, there was a fresh-water pool, in the hotel courtyard.

Gayle would remind Eric of how young he was. Everybody had been telling him that he was too young to take the Boards. That probably had weighed against him in the orals. Nancy — No! She was speaking for Gayle. And *Gayle* really believed it had. But he could try again in a year or two, after he'd practiced or in some way acquired experience of his own.

Thinking in this manner, she walked along the beach, up to the breakwater, then out upon it.

Did she want her sister to be skilled in handling Eric's disappointment? Did she want her to know just what to say to the man, how to touch him, how to comfort and reassure him, how to patch up his pride in himself?

Yes. Yes, she really did want that. Because Eric's hurt was Nancy's, and she must want

Gayle to come through at this time.

For a long hour she sat on the rocks, then decided that she was hungry — she had skipped lunch — and she could be offering some help and advice to Gayle.

She was more knowledgeable about medical things; she understood Eric's position much better than Gayle possibly could. She could tell her . . .

Or should she, Nancy, talk again to Eric? She already had suggested research — which he would do anyway. It was his real medical interest. But there were other things she could find to advise. Things that Eric should do.

She supposed the London position was washed up, but he could go away, to a different hospital, a different city. Away from his "failure." It really had not been that, but Nancy was sure Eric felt that it was one.

It might be good, too, for him to get away from his family. That was one reason he had wanted to go to London. There he would not be the rich grandson of the rich, and well-known, Gregory Ritter. He had said he wanted to be on his own. This was his chance.

Any move would take Gayle away from Tim Dineen, too, but that scarcely could be mentioned to Gayle, and probably should not be to Eric.

Having reached the hotel, Nancy freshened herself, combed her hair, and smoothed her blouse and skirt, shook out her pale cashmere sweater and hung it from her shoulders. Then she went across the lobby to the boutique. Gayle was there, and, to Nancy's surprise, said yes, she should stop for lunch.

It was two o'clock. They could go to the Garden Court Room where cocktails were served at five, and special luncheons from one until three. A beautiful room, one whole glass wall looked out to the sea; hanging baskets were about, and tall trees in tubs — rubber trees, orange trees, oleanders — making it seem more garden than room. Service was excellent and unobtrusive. The sisters ordered the famous shrimp salad, a wreath of giant Louisiana shrimp, rosy pink, arranged on crisp bright lettuce, with a special dressing. Gayle said she wanted iced coffee. She had a headache.

Had Nancy heard what had happened to poor Eric?

Yes, she had. It was disappointing but — and Nancy repeated all the alternatives which she had been thinking about. Before she was finished, she was stopped by Gayle's ringed hand on her arm. She wore many rings, and at least six bracelets, Gayle did.

White bracelets edged in gold, a heavy gold one, three gold-wire ones . . .

"Don't worry about it, Nancy," she said warmly. "It's all been planned out. Someone was telling me that the English medical setup wasn't working very well . . ."

"Eric was not planning to be a part of the National Health Service," said Nancy coldly.

"Well, whatever. We had quite a conference an hour ago. Grampa, and all of us. Eric is going to take over the hotel, and run it. Uncle Eugene never wanted the job; he's a banker at heart, and will be glad to get back to his vaults and cashier desks and whatever. Grampa is delighted . . ."

She rattled on, while Nancy felt as if she'd been caught in an undertow. In time, Eric would be just as good as Grampa at running a hotel. He had the brains, the presence . . .

Nancy shook her head in shocked despair. After several attempts, she finally managed to break in on Gayle's chatter.

"What about his *medicine?*" she asked.

Gayle regarded her — almost as if *she* pitied Nancy. "What about it?" she asked blandly. "He evidently isn't good at it."

Nancy leaned toward her. "But he *is* good at it!" she declared. "That he passed those Board exams at all — He's young, and those examinations are difficult! I've seen men ten years older than Eric, good, established doctors, sweat blood over those tests. They —" Holding Gayle's attention by sheer force, she talked for ten minutes about the Specialty Board examinations. Written and oral. The need to have cases to report, the qualifications of the examiners . . . Gayle ate her shrimp, one by one, and she must have heard something of what Nancy was saying.

"Eat your lunch," she said finally.

"But, Gayle . . ."

"You've had your say. I admit your readiness to interfere. But don't do it, Nancy. Don't do it. You can go on being Goody Two-shoes, if that's what you think gets you wherever it is you want to be!" She was angry. Nancy picked up her napkin and pressed it to her lips.

Then she rose abruptly and left the restaurant, managing to thread her way between the tables. She did not look back. She supposed Gayle would sign the check.

What should she do now? Stop trembling, for one thing. Should she talk again to Eric? She was terribly afraid for him; he so evidently was in danger. Gayle would be the wrong wife for him, she would destroy him . . .

She went to the desk and asked for coins; she would call Tim. At least tell him what had happened to Eric, and what threatened. She need not mention Gayle's name. She looked at her watch. The doctor might be in surgery — but she would try.

Then she would go home and cry herself to sleep.

It took nearly half an hour to locate Dr. Dineen, and to bring him to the phone. At first he was just pleased to talk to Nancy. Then her tone of voice warned him . . .

"Has something happened, Nancy?" he asked.

Even his voice, thirty miles away, was comforting. So she told him. And he was shocked, too. About the Boards results, and much more by the hotel idea. Whose fool notion had that been? "No, don't tell me. I'm afraid I know."

Oh, dear. He said he was coming down. He would talk to Eric. And he certainly wanted to talk to Nancy. How about dinner? Yes, at the hotel. Would she mind just waiting on him? In the lobby, he supposed. He couldn't tell exactly when he'd leave the hospital. If he saw Eric — and he'd need to run up and check on Amy. "I'll say seven, but it may be later."

Of course she would wait. She told him

exactly where. There was a big chair, sort of in the corner . . .

She saw him come in and cross the lobby to the elevators. Tall, dark-haired, his light suit well-fitting, a man sure of himself and his accomplishments. That was about seven. He would come down within the half hour if all was well with Amy. And it was. Nancy had gone up there earlier. The nurse had told her how pretty Nancy looked in a pink dress, "with two pink rosebuds tucked into the knot of her hair."

"There's a dance downstairs," Nancy told Amy. "A senior prom for the College class." And she described the girls. The would-be sophisticated ones in bare-top black dresses, the nice, pretty ones in ruffled lawn or gingham. The far-out "boys" in rented Tuxedos. "Every color. But I like the boys best who wear just the old-fashioned white serge jackets, or dark blazers with white flannel slacks. There's to be a banquet, and dancing. You probably will hear the music if you keep the balcony doors open. No, I'm not going to the dance. But I do have a dinner date."

She went downstairs, seeing herself in the mirror of the elevator. "Goody Two-shoes," she said to that image.

Tim thought she looked fine. At least he

said so. Yes, he had seen Eric. At the hospital. The guy was really sunk. He told about the woman patient who had had to lose her foot. The news of the exams had come along with that. Yes, Tim had mentioned Gayle's idea about the hotel. "Sure it was Gayle! Who else? I told Eric to put it out of his mind. That he could not do it, if ever he had been serious about medicine."

"He's been serious, Tim."

"Well, if he hasn't been, that could explain why he failed to hit the top on the Boards." Saying that, Tim had looked grim.

"He's serious, Tim," she said again.

"I think he is, too. But if he plans to marry Gayle, maybe he should not be."

She'd rather marry you, thought Nancy, but she didn't speak out on that.

They ate their dinner in the main dining room of the hotel; the waiters knew them both well, and smiled at them. Tim had to ask for wine. "They don't know that you've grown up," he confided to Nancy.

"Then they are like my father. He thinks I am eight, and a bit backward for my age."

"I'm just beginning, myself, to realize that you are aging," he confessed. "Though doing it very well, I must say. Why didn't you tell us what was going on behind our backs?"

"You're being kind, because you know how upset I am about Eric."

"That was why I came down here. No, it wasn't. I came mainly to help him get his wheels back on the track. But the minute I saw you! You were sitting there in that big chair in your pretty pink dress, your straight, pretty legs and white slippers, and your skirt pulled down neatly the way a lady should do it — and all the way up to Amy's room, I said to myself, 'Nancy is a beautiful young woman!' See? No more 'girl' business. You are sweet and compassionate, but you have poise, too, Nancy, and knowledge about important things . . ."

He said more — much more. She was flustered and pleased, and thoroughly enjoying herself. He was, he said, going to give her a rush, now that he had the evening off.

"Don't you have housekeeping to do back in the city?" she teased.

"You peeked! Well, let's forget the breakfast dishes, and enjoy ourselves. Do you want to dance?"

There was a small string orchestra. At first, Nancy refused, then she agreed. And found that Tim was an excellent dancer.

"When did you learn, and when do you practice?" she asked.

He gave her an absurd answer, but she

thought about his saying she was "older," and she decided that *he* had times of seeming "younger." Certainly he was a great charmer. He found a half dozen things to do as part of his "rush." A *lei* of tiny orchids bought from the girl circulating in the dining room. A drive to the Point to see the rising full moon, and to watch a cruise ship cross its wide path. They talked about cruises, and ones they would like to take.

"To Norway," said Nancy.

Tim thought he would enjoy the Virgin Islands. Or the Mediterranean . . .

Dreams. But happy ones. Did Nancy want to go bowling?

"You should be getting back to your rounds, Doctor."

"That's the trouble with dating a nurse!"

Dating.

But he agreed that he should take her home. "After a wild ride," he promised. She giggled.

"You're not afraid of a wild ride with me?"

"No. I'm just realizing how well I know you, Tim. How much I've always liked you and trusted you."

He turned his head and kissed her cheek.

Nancy sat thoughtful. Now a sailboat was crossing the moon path. At the beginning of the evening, Tim's attentions to her — she fingered the flowers — those things had puzzled her. He should give time to Eric, he should stop to see Amy — but Nancy? Did she need his kindness? Did he think she did?

Gayle would be amused if she knew. She would be amused when she found out. And she always found out. Why had Tim . . . ?

But by then, watching the sailboat, still feeling his lips against her cheek, Nancy decided that his act, his pursuit — whatever it was — added up just to pure fun. And it was rapidly developing into a genuine thrill.

"What about that wild drive?" she nudged him.

"Do you want to leave our moon?" he asked.

"We have the same one on our beach at home."

"But there would have been no wild drive."

"For a half mile? In five minutes? Is that the best you can do?"

He pretended to be offended. "Just for that, I should drive you home to wash my dishes."

"Just for that, I'd love to go."

He turned in the car seat. "Would you really, Nancy?" he asked seriously.

She met his gaze bravely. "Of course. But then, I'd like to stay right where we are.

With all the other smooching couples."

"Ah-hah!" he had cried. "Smooching! That's the best idea we've had between us!"

She wouldn't have believed it, but he did cuddle her. He drew her into his embrace. He kissed her cheeks, he kissed her lips, he smoothed her hair, and he kissed her again. And her hair escaped from its knot, the pins and the rosebuds fell to the car floor —

Then he sighed. "Oh, Nancy, Nancy! If I just could . . ."

She stopped groping for the tortoiseshell hairpins; she put her head down against his shoulder. "We'd better take that wild ride," she told him dreamily.

He tilted her face up into the light. He kissed her again, then moved back to his place behind the wheel. His face once more was his usual smooth, controlled countenance.

Chapter 10

It was an interlude. For both of them. Each of them had known it was just that. But it had been fun, too. Even now, remembering it, Nancy could feel her cheeks turn pink and her pulse begin to race.

She could not remember if the drive back to the hotel had been "wild" or not. The hotel was jumping with the senior dance. The music thumped and keened into the night air; Nancy entered the lobby, walking on air. Everyone could see she was on cloud nine.

Gayle saw it. And she spoke roughly to her sister. "For heaven's sake, Nancy!" she cried. "Go fix your lipstick, it's all over your face! And some boy's, too, I'd suspect."

Though she knew that Tim had brought her sister to the parking area. That was what angered her. For years she had considered Tim Dineen her property. She, too, was not ready to acknowledge that Nancy had "grown up." For all sorts of reasons, that frightened her. She had had a hard day . . .

Now Nancy could figure that out. But at

the time, she could only be shocked at the way Gayle flew at Tim and made a scene right there in the lobby. A bad scene.

Now Nancy could close her eyes and see it all. The people about — the three black dancers from the supper club act — they'd been wearing loose white shirts, skin-tight black trousers. There were tourists, mouths open, a couple from the senior dance, giggling and pretending to be shocked. Gayle in her slick black dress, held up only by the two-inch band of satin ribbon tied at the back of her throat. The sparkle of a huge pin not quite so bright as the light in her angry eyes.

Tim had stood quietly, not answering one thing she screamed at him. His face was as quiet as his hands.

"I would have shut her up with my two hands," Nancy now said aloud.

The hotel security man had approached, saying, "Something disturbing you, Miss Colburn?" And then Eric stepped up to her. Eric in a light blue jacket. He had put his arm around Gayle's shoulders and had spoken, not to her especially, but to those who stood around.

He'd made a neat little speech about how fine it was for Gayle to take such good care of her little sister.

Nancy, at the time, was speechless with rage. Especially at him. "If I had known the right words!" she said now, again clenching her fists in fury.

But that night she had simply walked away. She had gone out again, through the parking lot doors, stalking like a wooden soldier; and she had gone home.

That had been on Wednesday. Tuesday? Anyway, she had next seen Tim Dineen on Saturday night. No, it was on Friday. Down on the beach, talking to Gayle. About Nancy? More probably about Eric. Telling her, as Nancy had tried to do, that Eric needed a lot of loyalty just now. Maybe trying to tell her what to say to the poor guy.

Nancy, that Friday evening, had been hurt to see him there with Gayle, talking to her so earnestly. On Friday evening she still was in an opalescent daze from the "rush" he had given her.

But it was then, seeing him with Gayle, that she had begun to question why he had done that. Was he comforting Nancy, or, maybe, himself, for the turn things were taking? Gayle about to marry Eric . . .

For several minutes, Nancy considered this idea. And came up with some questions about herself and her feeling for Eric. Her family had been right. She had had a long,

long crush on the handsome, sweet-natured man.

But now the crush was gone. Blown away with the breeze. He had made her so furious by what he had said there in the lobby . . . At her next opportunity she would set him straight about her need for protection. Especially from Gayle. And most especially against Tim.

Tim. She got up, kicked the stool away from the metal door. She walked about the cell, and found herself beating her clenched fists against the wall.

For heaven's sake!

There had been interruptions during the morning. The doctor had come in and asked her how she was. He had offered to send her a glass of iced tea, which she appreciated. He had talked to her some about her work as a surgical assistant. Just how far did her training take her in her help to the surgeon? Was she something like a paramedic?

He might have had some motive behind his curiosity. She would not consider that.

Mr. Heser and Mr. Eskridge had come back, but Nancy had not felt like answering any more questions. She had told them all she knew, she said. They asked if she had been treated well, and she said she supposed she had been. They told her again that she was being held for a hearing, that she had not been charged with any crime.

It was while talking to them that the idea struck her. "I don't want to listen to any more arguments!" she told the men tensely. "I want to get *out* of here!"

To go to Tim, to talk to him, to explain . . . What?

That nothing could ever come of an orchid *lei,* a "wild ride," or even of their smooching. Even if things developed, even if he "loved" Nancy, and she loved him — which was very likely already a fact — nothing whatever could come of it. Because in that case, no one — literally *no* one! — would ever believe that she had not . . .

Her thoughts drifted away; she sat down and looked glumly at her feet. *That she had not killed Amy.*

Lunch, or more probably dinner, was brought to her. She sat looking at the tray. Midmorning, the sun had left her window, and now clouds seemed to be gathering. Too bad, on a weekend, she thought mechanically. All her life, a rainy weekend had meant bad business for the hotel, the beach, and the town.

She herself rather liked to see the rollers

come in, faster, and faster . . . and the surf rise . . .

Again she paced about the room, desperate to get out, to feel the sand, the wind, the sea spray on her face, the taste of salt on her lips.

She sat down and made a sandwich of the thick bread and the chicken. She did not taste the pale gravy or the potatoes. She chewed the sandwich, and tried to read Mr. Heser's book.

In the mood she was in, her food would probably make her ill. Which would be the last straw!

When the tray was taken, she lay down on the cot and stared at the ceiling. To dispel the "mood," she would think of more pleasant things. Of the night with Tim, the way they had danced — of the moon off the Point, and —

It was no use. All she could think of was where she was, the noises from the jail, and about how she had got there. She thought of the way word had come to her of Amy's death. Her mother had told her. Nancy had been really shocked. And sorry. But from her present position, it seemed that she had been positively lighthearted about it all. She had dressed up and gone blithely off to the hotel —

To tell Tim that now he was free to marry Gayle. Why had she *done* such a thing?

Because she felt the occasion required her to be big-hearted. She had known even then that she did not want him to marry Gayle.

And Tim, listening to her, had told her —

Did she believe him? That he was in love with Gayle's sister?

She did not think she had, actually, taken the declaration seriously. And after that, she had decided, once again, to go back to work the next day. Vacations well might not be for her. She did better when she stuck to a routine of work, and sleep, and work again. With maybe a movie or a game of tennis with one of the other nurses for diversion. Maybe a date now and then. It was not a bad life. Better than the vacation she'd been having at the Beach.

If she had thought, if she had *dreamed*, that it would wind up with her arrested for murder, and in jail —

Oh, yes! She had not been arrested! She was being *held for questioning*. But she *was* in jail, had slept in jail, she wore the jail's awful clothes! And she was being held for questioning only because she seemed to know more about the case than anyone else. The case of murder! What was there to know, more than that poor Amy Dineen had died in a pool of blood from an artery someone, presumably Nancy Colburn, had cut?

Well, yes, she knew how to cut an artery — or a vein. But she certainly had not cut one on Amy! She — she —

The whole experience was incredible! And why couldn't someone else see that it was incredible? Her parents — Tim — if he knew what was going on? Eric, if he knew —

Would they believe her? Or that Eskridge fellow who seemed to have the power to put her in this place, to have her fingerprints taken — She didn't mind that, except for what doing it here in jail implied. Her fingerprints were on record. As a nurse, registered. As a technician, registered.

Weren't they the same fingerprints? She supposed they had looked for needletracks on her arms, too!

Stiffly, she lay on the bed and listened for footsteps along the hall. She was ready to spring at anyone who came near, and prove to them . . .

Someone would come. Someone. Tim . . .

From sheer weariness, her eyelids drooped, she sighed, and slept.

And Tim did come. The cell door was unlocked, he came in and was standing over her; his forefinger touched the tears still damp on her cheek.

She sprang up to her feet. She backed away. She could not believe . . .

"Tim!" she said hoarsely.

He put his hand on her arm. A warm hand, comforting, and strong. Then he held out the bundle which he was carrying.

"What is it?" she asked, brushing her hair back from her face. She had slept just long enough to be fuzzy-headed.

"It's a raincoat and hood. You'll need it." She still did not understand.

"I am taking you home," he said.

She stared at him. "You mean I can leave?"

"As soon as you change your clothes. It seems they want to keep what you are wearing." By then, he was smiling at her.

"But —" She still did not understand. "You mean — Did someone put up bail?"

Now where did she get that term? Why hadn't she expected — Grampa would do it, or Eric. Her own father — He would mortgage his — his —

"No bail," Tim was saying firmly. He said it a couple of times. "There never was an arrest, Nancy . . ."

"That's what you think!" she told him. She was feeling better. "Where are my clothes?" She took the raincoat.

"Down the corridor. The matron has

them." He was watching her closely. He opened the cell door and let her precede him.

She smiled up at him faintly. "I'm glad you came," she said softly.

"Well, of course I came. Here's the matron."

Nancy changed quickly. Afterward the matron told how that Colburn girl had said she disliked putting on underclothes for the second time without their being laundered. "But she managed to do it. She seemed right glad to do it!"

The silky raincoat was new, and Tim said Nancy looked as cute as a button in it.

"Did you buy it?" she asked. It was a red and blue plaid coat; there was a hood to pull up over her hair. He smiled at her, and turned to sign something at the desk.

"Good-bye, Miss Colburn," said the policeman there.

"Good-bye . . ." She and Tim went out into the soft warm rain.

Tim put her into his car, and got in himself. Then he bent over and kissed her cheek.

"Tell me," she said. "How did I ever get in that place, and how did you ever get me out of it? And the raincoat is lovely. I'll pay you back."

"You couldn't afford to," he said solemnly, but there were crinkles at the corners of his eyes. His good, dark eyes.

"You may have to go into court tomorrow," he said, "so that your case can be *nolle-prossed*."

"For heaven's sake —"

"Don't you read detective stories?"

"I never will again. And if you don't tell me . . ."

"I know. You won't pay me for the raincoat."

"That's right. So talk. How did you get me out of the crazy mess I was into?"

"Because it was a crazy mess." He started the car and waited for a chance to drive out into the street. "The whole thing was complete nonsense. Why they should have even questioned you —"

"Because — I figured that out. Because I know more than anyone else what had happened."

"*Agggh!*" He sounded angry. "Nobody knew anything! This was a matter of eager-beaver police, a talkative nurse, and something your sister said as a joke. When Ritter found out what they had done to you . . ."

"Did he know I'd been put in jail?"

"Not until this morning. Yesterday — last

228

night — he had a very difficult case at the hospital —"

"And of course he was preoccupied with his disappointment about the Boards."

"Yes, but mainly it was the case. He's too good a doctor to let anything but a case take up all of his attention. And for an orthopedist, to lose a foot unnecessarily is such a case. But, anything — when he did find out, he went to work. He had pronounced Amy's death, and he did think she had cut her own wrist, that she had bled to death. But when he found you were being held, he convinced the police, or whomever it took, that you would not do such a clumsy job. Her wrist was mangled, Nancy. She had sawed away at it. Even the nurse had told Eric that she could use her right hand."

"Yes, she could. And she did it with that nail file?"

"That was their idea. Eric thought she had managed. Before he knew that I had insisted on an autopsy, he thought that was what killed her. When he saw the autopsy report, he agreed that the attempt could have sent her blood pressure sky-high, and she died. The b.p. part of it could have happened at any time during the past ten years. Her heart was strong enough, with the care she had, to survive . . . And then, all at once, it wasn't strong enough."

"You mentioned Gayle . . ."

"I hope you will think she was just being flip. She *knew* you wouldn't do such a thing! And actually that is what she said to the policeman or to somebody who let the bloodhounds loose after you. As I say, a tremendous mistake, and nonsense, from the start. But Ritter and I felt that we had enough expert evidence to — I believe the term is 'to spring you.' So we went to the District Attorney . . ."

"D.A.," Nancy murmured.

Those same smile wrinkles sprayed out from the corner of his right eye. "And," he continued, "we found your attorney there before us. Because, it seems, there is a law that says that a prisoner must be released after being held for twenty hours if no warrant has been issued during that time. No charges had been filed, or warrant issued, so — after some inevitable red tape, I came to get you!"

"They wouldn't believe me," said Nancy faintly, watching her home come "down the street toward the car." A fantasy remaining from her childhood.

But there it was, spreading out beyond the flower beds, low and inviting, rain glistening on its roof, the long windows, the strong beams and the stone and brick walls . . .

"Home looks wonderful," she sighed.

Chapter 11

Her father came outside to greet her, and then, for a minute, could not speak. He held her close and patted her shoulder. "Bless you!" he finally managed.

Blinded by tears, Nancy stooped to greet the family dog who was jumping about in pleasure.

The rest of the family were in the living room, Gayle and Eric in the woven cane chairs at one end, her mother on the couch. Nancy went straight to her, and in her turn was unable to speak. She slipped out of the raincoat and said something silly about Tim's buying it. "I wouldn't have minded getting wet," she said, accepting the Kleenex which Eric brought to her. She sat down, and the cat jumped into her lap, nibbling at her hand.

Nancy petted him and looked about the room as if seeing it for the first time. A tiny fire burned on the hearth, and the rain slapped in gusts against the wide window. Through its glass she could see a Japanese print glimpse of the ocean, as green as clear glass, with little white-tipped waves arranged symmetrically.

Her father sat down in the armchair nearest to the fire. Tim came in and stood beside the other chair.

"He looks," said Nancy, "the way he does when he's finished scrub. He stands there with his arms dripping water, he takes — snatches! — a towel from the tray, and wipes his hands, and he checks on everything in o.r."

He's doing that now, checking, she thought. His eyes see the ocean, and me, his eyes soften when he looks at poor Mom. He nods to Dad, and his muscles tighten when he looks at Gayle and at Eric. Gayle's pretty green and white dress is wasted on him.

They all looked at Tim, waiting for him to speak. He had things to say, Nancy knew. He stood tall, thoughtful. His dark hair was smooth, his clothes well-cut — a light gray suit, blue shirt and dark blue tie with closely set white dots. Nancy took a deep breath. She knew him well, she knew what he was thinking, how he was feeling; she could almost feel the touch of his strong hands, one half clenched at his side, the other ready to gesture, forefinger pointed.

He would say . . .

He did say.

"I feel that I owe all of you an apology for the treatment which Nancy has received in the past twenty-four hours," he said formally. Briefly his eyes flashed across her face.

How did she look? In her somewhat rumpled dress, her hair not properly brushed, certainly not pinned back from her face. No makeup, no lipstick. She bent her head over the black cat.

"Certainly," Tim was saying. "That treatment was not what I would have wanted for her. Though, not in self-defense so much as explanation for the delay — I do wish, the next crime she commits, that Nancy might choose some other time than Saturday and Sunday of a weekend."

Her head lifted. "It's not a joke, Tim!" she said sharply.

"No, it is not, Nancy. But it is going to be better if all of us can learn to think of this as rather amusing." He smiled at her. "There has, fortunately, been very little except word-of-mouth publicity about this — er — the apprehension and — er — incarceration of Miss Colburn. Though I can tell you that I have already seen to it that there will be full publicity as to the findings of the autopsy by which the causes of my wife's death were determined."

"You didn't do that post, did you, Dineen?" Eric asked.

"No, I did not. But I did ask for it. And it was performed as quickly as possible yesterday afternoon. I was fully informed of the findings." He told of the "superficial wound" on the wrist. "Messy, but not fatal. Though the excitement and the real effort over inflicting it could readily explain the rise of blood pressure, the hemorrhage, and the death. Those, on the record, explain it all."

Mrs. Colburn moved. "Why don't you sit down, Doctor?" she asked kindly. "I am sure you too have had a bad couple of days. We do condole with you in Amy's death. I understand there was no funeral."

Tim did sit down then, but he leaned forward, his hands clasped between his knees. "There was an almost immediate burial," he said slowly, "after the autopsy. No funeral, no visitation, no flowers . . ." He seemed to speak impersonally.

Then he straightened and sat back in the chair. Nancy wished it had a high back so that he could rest his head.

"You see," he said, "My wife — Amy — really died ten years ago. On the day that I was told, and accepted the fact, that recovery would be impossible, that a meaningful life would forever be impossible to her. And I grieved. Perhaps some think those things are more easily understood and accepted by doctors, by men trained to know the full implications."

"They are not," said Eric, his voice gruff.

Tim glanced at him and nodded. "No, they are not," he agreed. "But when I had to accept what amounted to a life sentence for that young woman, I grieved. I grieved terribly. But you know, Mrs. Colburn, that acute grief cannot survive for ten years. Sorrow, yes, and regret. I am sorry now for Amy as she was ten years ago, but grief for the — for the woman she had become, no. I could not weep now. I welcome her release. I do not rejoice at her release, but I do accept it as a good thing."

"You were very good to her," said Nancy's mother.

"No," said Tim slowly. "Not good. The care of her became a duty only. It's all a part of the fact that grief, even despair, have for so long passed away. I hope you may understand . . ."

"We do understand, Tim," said Nancy's father warmly, "and we still say you were wonderful."

Tim got to his feet and walked to the big window where he stood looking out at the rain and at the sea. "Not wonderful at all," he said sternly. "I have hated that I had to live so. With no freedom, no —" He swung around. "Even the money part," he cried loudly. "That was a real burden at first. At first, of course — I was an intern — and the hospital was generous, the doctors were generous — but there still were expenses. Terrible bills. I went in debt even while I was spending every cent I could make. That was a real load.

"When the hospital could no longer give her custodial care, I brought her here. I could not afford it, but I did that. I worked very hard at my profession. Not because of a real love for the work I did, but because it paid well enough for me to give Amy shelter, comfort, nursing and pleasant surroundings, fresh, good air. Gradually I paid off my debts, though now I am broke. Oh, I have a little money in the bank. A few thousand dollars. But I have hated every cent, every minute, every backache it has cost me to get where I am. I do hope you understand what I am saying about the things you call wonderful."

"We do understand, Tim," said Mr. Colburn. "And you did not need to tell us those things for us to understand them."

"It's all behind you now," said his wife.

Tim took the dark blue handkerchief from his pocket and patted his forehead. Then he came to sit beside Nancy on the couch.

"Yes," he agreed. "It's over. Now —" He looked across at the girl in the green and white dress. "I have a thing or two to say on other matters. First, to Gayle."

Nancy looked up at him in alarm. "I think I'll go brush my hair," she said hastily.

His hand held her arm. "It's the time to get these things said, once and for all, Nancy. Then they may be forgotten and we — all of us — can go on with our lives."

Nancy stole a swift glance at Gayle. Her smile had faded from bright receptiveness to watchful apprehension.

"I don't think Gayle was — was —"

"She never actually *does* things, Nancy. Do you, Gayle?" His voice was harsh, his manner stern. "But she loves to make mischief. Don't you, Gayle?"

She flipped an end of her bright brown hair. "I haven't the least idea what you are talking about," she said.

"You use people, Gayle. You play a constant game of checkers with the people about you. You say a word here, a word there. You pretend to tell a joke when actually you are accusing someone. I don't like it

237

when you use Nancy or me in your game."

Again Nancy looked alarmed. "She hasn't hurt me, Tim," she said earnestly.

"A flip word from her yesterday sent the police after you."

"What did she say?" asked Eric, his question only curious.

"She could tell you. I shan't. I'll only say that she thought Nancy and I were a real menace to her plans with you."

Eric looked blank. "I cannot imagine . . ." he began.

But Nancy broke in. "Why you, Tim? Maybe she thought, as I did, that you owed her something, that now —"

"Now what?" he asked. Softly. He was looking, not at Nancy but at Gayle.

"Oh, I don't know!" Nancy cried. "I just wish things could be more simple!"

"They almost never are, my dear," said her father, "and they won't be. Not so long as you have beautiful women like your sister playing on the far side of the net."

Everyone in the room turned to look at him in surprise. He laughed. "I don't run a department in a girls' school without learning a few things myself," he assured his family and the two young men. "I remember when Tim Dineen first came here to Peter's Beach. We all felt sorry for the young doctor, because of his invalid wife. Gayle was at the age to offer him real sympathy. Nancy was too young, and that bothered her. And for years afterward she felt that Tim should be grateful for Gayle's assistance to him. Perhaps she feels that still, though, all along, she has taken the situation much too seriously."

Tim stood up, Eric slumped lower in his low chair. Gayle stood up, too. "Now I think I'll brush *my* hair!" she said firmly, and walked out of the room.

"Mr. Colburn," said Tim. "You amaze me."

"Yes, I know I do. I may say that I think you have always handled Gayle extremely well."

"I came to know her well," said Tim grimly. "For instance, our latest conflict has been over an ultimatum I gave her. That she was to tell Eric of our brief intimacy seven years ago."

"Did she tell you?" Mr. Colburn asked that befuddled young man.

"No, sir. I don't think so. At least, this is the first time I've heard of that."

The three men laughed. "She did tell me," said Eric, "that Dineen had always taken advantage of Nancy's youth and inexperience."

This brought Nancy to her feet, and now it was Veronica who pulled her back to the couch. "You're not going to let her get to you, are you, Nancy?" she asked calmly.

The men really did laugh then, but Nancy was still upset. "I don't know," she cried, "why men let women do the sort of thing you're accusing Gayle of doing! They're not fools in other matters."

Tim sat down beside her on the couch. "It's not a matter of being fools even in this 'thing,' as you call it. This 'matter.' What you women don't want to acknowledge, though you know it as a fact, is that a woman as beautiful as Gayle is, and as desirable, can have and do almost anything she wants."

Nancy sat shaking her head. "I know just one thing," she said. "I am glad I am not beautiful."

At once, everyone protested this. "You're a nice girl," said her mother. "And you are too pretty."

Tim was more specific, and spoke at greater length. He said she was more than pretty. In many ways she was even more beautiful than Gayle. As a rosebud was more beautiful than the full-open flower. "Your honesty shows through and gives a shine to all your other qualities. Really, Nancy, you *are* more beautiful than Gayle is."

"Oh, forget it," she said crossly. "I don't want to be compared to Gayle. And I wish you and Eric would go home."

Eric stood up, but Tim did not. "I'll try not to compare you to anyone," he agreed. "I love you too much, Nancy, ever to want to hurt you."

She was weary, and she wasn't ready, just then, to hear such a declaration. "Thank you," she said primly.

Mrs. Colburn was looking at Mr. Colburn. "I think I'll fix a little supper," said Nancy's mother.

"I'm going to bring Gayle back in here," said Eric.

Tim looked at the Professor. "Let's help with that supper," he said.

Chapter 12

For twenty minutes, perhaps a half hour, there was much moving about between kitchen and dining room; its windows opened on more flower beds. Nancy took a shower and changed into a fresh dress. Yellow and white striped. She pinned her hair securely on top of her head.

Eric's voice rumbled from Gayle's room, and then, looking cross, he came out to help Tim put ice and lemon slices into the tall glasses of tea. The two doctors were actually talking shop, about some woman whom another doctor had made a cripple. "Cut the femoral artery!" said Eric loudly. "I learned to identify that in med school."

Tim said something, and Eric laughed. They both laughed.

"We have more talking to do," Andrew Colburn told his wife. "We could be having two weddings, Mother."

"Perhaps. One for sure."

"I like Tim."

His wife nodded, counting the plates which she had set out on the counter. The perfume of baking rolls filled the air. "Did Eric let Gayle . . . ?" she murmured.

"No, he said she was to stay right here. This time she'll do it."

They ate supper. The sliced tomatoes and mounds of salmon salad, the hot rolls and butter; they drank the iced tea and acclaimed the wedges of cherry pie.

"I was so worried about Nancy," Mrs. Colburn explained, "I had to keep busy today."

"And you keep busy by baking delicious, fattening pies," said Gayle, again able to smile brightly.

And they talked.

During the meal, Nancy had had little to say, and the others, being tactful, allowed her to be silent. Gayle had chattered, Mr. Colburn talked about flowers that stood up well under rain, and those that collapsed into the mud.

Eric said that Mrs. Colburn should teach the hotel pastry chef how to make cherry pie, and Nancy spoke up on that.

"Couldn't a jail afford to give us prisoners salmon salad?" she asked.

For some reason this broke the film of tact and kindness that had been holding them.

"Was it really bad?" Eric asked her.

"The bad part," said Nancy readily, "was

that nobody seemed to believe me when I said —"

"They thought you had done it," said Gayle. "I thought you probably had."

"You must have known you were being ridiculous!"

"No, I didn't think I was." Her smile was as smooth as a silken fold of her pretty dress. "I thought you had decided it would be a way to free Tim so that I could marry him and you could get Eric. That wasn't ridiculous, was it, Nancy?"

"The only trouble, Gayle," Nancy replied, almost indifferently, "was that, for seven years, I have been growing up; you haven't noticed."

"And now you don't love Eric any more!"

"Oh, sure. I love him like the brother I never had. He's great." She smiled across the table at Eric, who flushed a little and returned her smile.

Tim cleared his throat. "Tell me, Ritter," he said. "Your suggestion that the hotel chef learn how to make Mrs. Colburn's cherry pie — that wouldn't indicate that you are seriously considering a change in careers, would it? That you might take over the management of the hotel?"

Eric pushed his chair back from the table and smoothed his hand back over his hair.

"Dineen," he said, "for the past few days, I don't really think I've considered anything seriously. Maybe not even sanely. The thing is, about the hotel, which, incidentally, I consider a great institution, and one which should be preserved . . ."

"Hey, hey!" said Tim.

"Yes. Well, the thing is that Grampa *is* aging."

"Did Grampa know I was in jail?" Nancy broke in to ask.

Eric smiled at her. "I don't believe so, darling. I hope he did not."

She sat back. "So do I. Go on, Eric. I'm sorry I interrupted."

"It's all right," said Eric. "I was going to say that Parmeley — Uncle Eugene, as I am supposed to say, but usually don't —"

"You don't like him," said Gayle.

"Oh, now, look! We don't have much in common. But — Well, anyway, Uncle Eugene does not like running the hotel business. He's used to being an accountant, a bookkeeper. Something of the sort. A bank teller . . ."

"A bank *president!*" said Gayle firmly.

"Yes, I believe he is. Anyway," Eric continued, "he wants to sit at a desk where he need not speak to anyone, where certainly he does not need to meet guests. All kinds of guests."

"I don't suppose," said Tim, "that he has an allergy to the Ritter money which, filthy or otherwise, those guests pour into the family coffers? And eventually, I suppose, into his wife's pockets."

Eric shrugged. "That states one side of the business. The other side is that he does not like being in the hotel business. He has boys coming along, but they are still too young. Naturally, I have been considered. But that won't work, either. I chose to study medicine rather than business administration."

"I can sympathize with you," said Mr. Colburn. "I cannot see you taking over the management of that hotel. Or any hotel. Dressed impeccably — Well, you do dress that way, of course, but not in a dark club coat and a striped tie. You don't sit in your grandfather's lobby chair, with an eagle eye on everything that goes on in that great lobby, supervising the people who go in and out, the clerks, the chefs, the maids and the garage men — And besides all that supervision which must cover a lot of people, there would be the continuous guest room and suite inspections, the purchase of things like new carpeting and dining-room silver, and maids' uniforms, and bellhops' shoes. You may not have the instinct to determine special guests in need of special attention . . ."

Gayle sat, her chin on her clenched fist, and listened to her father. "*I* could run your hotel," she said quietly, clearly.

Nancy laughed, then stopped when she saw that the others were taking the suggestion seriously.

"You can't keep your room and your closet in order," said her mother. "But you have done extremely well with the boutique."

"She has a genius for making others do what she wants," said Mr. Colburn. He and his wife seemed well pleased with the idea.

"She's one to crack the whip, all right," said Tim.

"She could run it," said Eric, "while Grampa is still able to tell her what is needed."

Mrs. Colburn looked stricken. "But what about the wedding we announced ten days ago?"

"What about it?" said Gayle blandly.

"But if you marry Eric, would he want . . . ?"

"I'm going to London," said Eric quietly.

This was news indeed. Everyone talked about it at once. When was that decided? When would he go? Wasn't it what he had so wanted?

Tim leaned forward, his eyes bright. "That's what happened to your thirty-six-hour duty," he decided. "So, tell us."

Eric answered them all. He had had an overseas call that day in response to his cable telling about the result of the Board exams. "I still know more than they do about the new equipment and the research they want."

"Will you be a senior consultant?" Nancy asked.

"I don't know."

"The pay is nothing," said Gayle.

Eric shrugged. He would leave this next week, he said. "I put my resignation from the hospital back into effect immediately after the call."

"So if Gayle . . ." said Gayle's father.

"Yes, sir." He had told her the news earlier. "While Mrs. Colburn was baking the pie."

For some excited reason this made everyone laugh.

". . . and if Gayle really does want to manage the hotel . . ."

The talk went on, but Nancy scarcely heard a word of it. There would be no marriage, and Eric would be free. Though, probably in London, he would work very hard at medicine.

And Tim!

She looked at him. He was talking fast about something, teasing Gayle, who was flushed and excited, and beautiful.

But Nancy no longer wanted him to marry Gayle.

And Eric?

Oh, she just did not know!

Watching Tim, she realized suddenly and contritely how very tired the man must be. In the past two days, the things he had done! Amy — and Nancy's problems — Yet, here he was, as fresh as an intern going off thirty-six-hour duty.

Abruptly, she stood up.

"Maybe no one cares," she said, "but I think we all should go back to work. I should, and Tim — he must be bone-tired! Eric should be packing his bags. Everybody! Mother and Dad, Grampa, and Mr. Parmeley at the hotel. Unless Gayle means to take over his job tonight. Let's all go to work, instead of sitting around talking about it!"

"Sit down, Nancy," said their mother finally.

"The rain has stopped. I want to go to the beach, but I'll help you get things cleared away here first."

Tim touched her arm. "Sit down, as your mother said."

She hesitated, but finally she did sit on the

edge of her chair. She didn't think she could *bear* any more talk!

Her mother was asking Eric when he must leave for England.

"I promised I would be there this week."

"Then we'll have to get busy with the wedding. Nancy, your dress should be shortened. If you're to be the brides-maid . . ."

"How can I be a bridesmaid?" she asked crossly. "I'm a convict!"

Everyone laughed, more or less politely. "You didn't make a very good convict," Tim told her.

"I understand," said Mr. Colburn, "that the state is dropping all charges. That there will be no trial because there is no case."

"I have to be in court tomorrow."

"A formality."

"I'm also supposed to be back at work to-morrow. My vacation is over."

"You said you had until Wednesday."

"Well . . . if I use some sick leave time."

"Then you are to use it."

Chapter 13

Nancy helped her mother clear away the supper dishes. Tim and Eric went off together. To the hospital, Gayle thought. "They didn't consult me."

She herself soon disappeared.

"Put on a coat," her mother told Nancy when they had everything tidy, "if you're going to the beach."

"A sweater," Nancy agreed. "You don't mind if I go? I have missed the beach."

"I know. You've always loved it. Your Daddy used to call you his sand dollar."

"I'm glad he stopped doing *that!*" said Nancy. She kissed her mother. "I'm sorry I've been a problem."

Her mother looked at her, astonished. "You've never been a problem in your life!" she declared firmly.

"Then I'd better not start now, had I? I'll be back by dark."

The rain clouds were breaking up, the late sun was gleaming upon them, making all sorts of pictures for Nancy to watch. The receding tide, and the rain, had smoothed the sand into glistening stretches that shone like silver. Nancy kicked off her sandals and, holding them in her hand, went to the ocean's edge where the little waves coming in could curl about her ankles.

Tim Dineen found her there, one of the only two figures silhouetted tiny and black against the burnished stretch of the beach. He had changed into loose white slacks and a turtleneck sweat shirt of a nondescript gray. He called to her from ten feet away. "I didn't want to startle you," he said.

Nancy, without turning, held out her hand. "Did you and Eric get things straightened out?" she asked.

"We looked at his amputee. Boy, what a malpractice case that woman has! She need not have lost her foot. But with Ritter in England . . ."

"When does he leave?" They were walking slowly along the sand.

"He's made a flight reservation for Thursday."

A reservation?

"He said something about your, maybe, working for him. With him."

Nancy looked interested. "Did he, really?"

"I don't want you to do it, Nancy."

She stopped, then turned to look at him. "Why not?"

"Because London is a long, long way from where I am working."

"Oh." She began to walk again. "Don't you want to put on your shoes?"

"I like to squash in wet sand."

"You can get a cut. "

"I know. But I still like it. Tim, do you think I am still in love with Eric. The way Gayle said."

"I hope you're over any youthful crushes."

"Well, maybe I hope so, too. And I think I am, where Eric is concerned. Though he's the only real crush I ever had . . ."

"What about me?"

"Oh, you were always different. But Eric — I've been 'adoring' him for so long — and I'm such a loyal person — I don't change easily. I know he's more like a brother, but — I think I may be in a rather terrible situation with him."

"How is it terrible?"

"Well, if I'd agree to go to England and work with him, he might think I expected him to — well — return my feeling for him. And that feeling might grow, too! You know it might."

"I well understand that it might," said Tim. "What about Gayle?"

"You mean, what if he does marry her? That's another way my feeling for Eric may be terrible."

"Maybe you have just got into the habit of loving the guy, safe in the knowledge that you couldn't ever have him."

Nancy stopped dead where she was. "Are you turning psychiatrist?" she asked.

He seized her arm. "No," he assured her. "I'm busy enough being a surgeon. That's why I want to be sure you are going back to my o.r. on Thursday. I'll pick you up early that morning."

"But —"

"I took this week off. I'll go to court with you tomorrow. I'll see that Ritter gets his affairs packed up. I'll haunt you for a couple of days. Then I'll take you back to the city, and we'll both get to work. The main thing is, sweetheart, I want you where I can persuade you — Oh, maybe it will take as much as six weeks — but I want to bet that in that time you will be convinced that you love me. Maybe I've already told you that a busy doctor has to concentrate his courtship. Here, hang on, and put on your shoes."

The shoes on, they walked toward the hotel.

"How about that bet?" He nudged her.

She laughed. Excitement was rising like bubbles within her. "I never bet except on a sure thing, Doctor."

"Nor me, nor me. Do you want to go

home now, or into the hotel?"

"Are you staying at the hotel?"

"I moved out. I have a cubby in the residents' quarters at the hospital. I plan to continue as consultant there."

"That's good. Maybe I can hook rides down here whenever you come."

"That's part of my plan."

And Nancy laughed aloud. "You're wonderful," she told him.

"That's what I mean. I grow on a person."

"What about Eric and this London job?" she asked.

"Are you changing the subject?"

"No. I want to continue that. But I also want to know about Eric. I had thought, if he didn't make diplomate . . ."

"I believe that specific was largely in his own mind, that there had been no stipulation. He told me that when he talked to the people over there about passing the Boards, but not making the top rating, they insisted that they still wanted him."

"I'm really glad. Do you think . . . ?"

"That Gayle will go with him? No, I don't. Girls as popular as Gayle often do not marry until they are older, if they marry at all. It's a matter of a riper and more luscious fruit always higher up on the matrimonial tree."

"Oh, my goodness!" said Nancy, pretending awe.

"Anything you want to know on the subject, just ask me."

"I'll do that. Gayle did seem fired up on the hotel management thing."

"She'd be good at it, too. She has all it takes. But there is one thing . . ."

"What's that?"

"Earlier, when I helped take some of Eric's gear from the hospital to the hotel — he had a lot! We borrowed one of the bellboys' dollies . . ."

"Why didn't you borrow a bellboy?"

"Because we didn't think of it, I guess. Anyway, when we came back, Eric's niece — a very pretty young girl, about seventeen, I'd say —"

"Barbara. Yes, she has a hard crush on Gayle."

"Does she? Well, that might complicate things."

"How?"

"Oh, when this Barbara was helping Eric and me, she babbled about having decided to stay on here at the Beach, go to school, but also work at learning how to run the hotel."

"My goodness!" said Nancy. "And she's Eric's cousin, not his niece. Her mother . . ."

"I know that. She was also saying that she hoped Gayle would help her learn."

"To do the job Gayle wants to do? Not in a hundred years!"

"Barbara is a Ritter."

"Now you know as well as I do that if Barbara threatens to push Gayle out of the management job which she wants . . ."

"Barbara wouldn't want to do that, would she?"

Nancy hooted. "She won't do it!" she said firmly. "Gayle isn't the girl to be pushed anywhere, by anybody!"

They slowly mounted the low brick steps which led to the wide terrace; they went between the urns of flowers, between the people who were standing about, and, to their surprise, as they went along the terrace, they came upon old Mr. Ritter — Grampa — a plaid cap on his head, a folded robe across his knees. He was using a wheelchair . . .

Nancy looked at Aim. "Isn't that . . . ?"

"Amy's chair. Yes. He asked to buy it."

"And you gave it to him."

"Well, the hotel has been very good to me. And the chair — our engineer at the hospital put all sorts of dual controls and gadgets into it —"

"But Gayle is still pushing it."

Gayle was. She was guiding the upholstered chair along the terrace, being gay — and attentive — to the old gentleman. Grampa was delighted, greeting everyone . . .

"I'll have to show him how to operate the thing himself," said Tim.

"I believe he already knows," drawled Nancy.

Tim turned sharply to look at her. "Cynicism from *you?*" he asked, shocked, or pretending to be.

"Gayle brings things out in me I scarcely know I have," Nancy told him.

"Yeah. She does in a lot of people. You don't suppose the old man . . . ?"

"Grampa's pretty foxy himself. Almost every woman around the hotel has tried to take Grandma's place with him."

"And you think maybe Gayle could succeed where others haven't? Luddy, you *are* cynical!"

"Realistic. But I have not yet decided whether Gayle *would* . . ."

"I really don't think she could go that far, Nancy. But I do suspect . . ."

"That Barbara should train for something other than hotel management." Nancy laughed. "Yes, she should. Because Gayle . . ."

As if she had heard her name, Gayle saw them, and called to them, waving.

"We'll have to speak to Grampa," Nancy whispered.

"Yes, of course." But they walked slowly. Gayle turned the chair and came toward them. Grampa was delighted to see them. He held Nancy's two hands, and told her about the chair. Tim had given it to him, he said. He knew that it had hand controls. "I can walk," he said, "but my feet swell. You're a nurse, aren't you, Nancy darling?"

"Yes, Grampa, but I work in the hospital. I work for Dr. Dineen."

"He's lucky. I'd like to have a nurse like you."

"Gayle's prettier."

"Maybe yes, maybe no. But one thing is sure. You're nicer. I always thought so when you were just little girls."

"You're right, Grampa," Gayle agreed. "Of course she's nicer."

Nancy nodded. "That makes it pretty unanimous, doesn't it? Because I am *sure* I am nicer!"

They all laughed, but Gayle, even as they laughed, was pushing Grampa on down the terrace. As they rounded the curve, she looked back at Nancy.

Tim reached for, and took, her hand.

"The air is getting very bad," he said gruffly. "Let's run away from here."

"Where shall we run?"

"It doesn't matter. Anywhere."

Not exactly running, they went across the terrace, they quickened their pace around the edge of the parking area, and they did begin to run down the street. Tim still held Nancy's hand in his, and when he slowed, she did.

"Is Eric going to be all right?" she asked, panting a little.

"He can take care of himself. Even if Gayle — If, with his money and his profession, he can't handle things, what could we ever do for the man?"

Nancy nodded. "I hope I don't really love him."

They had reached the walk between her father's rose beds. Low, shaded lights illuminated the bricks. Tim drew the girl close. "I'm going to show you that you don't love Eric," he promised. And he kissed her.

Nancy did not expect to sleep that night; she never had after a dance when a couple of the fellows had given her a rush. But she did sleep — soundly, dreamlessly. "Maybe it was the change from a jail cot," she told herself when she awoke. "Or maybe I'm getting old enough not to take these things seriously. After all, what's a kiss?"

It was a beautiful morning. She would go to the beach and be back well before nine, she promised her parents. Her father was going to court with her. Maybe Tim would be there. Oh, surely he would be. He had said . . .

A piece of toast in hand, she pulled on her beach robe, said, yes, she had shoes on, and she went out. The eastern sky was rosy pink, the sea was doing what Nancy called "sobbing," rising in slow swells that never rushed into shore, but lifted there and sank back . . . Sobbing.

She dropped her robe and sandals, lifted her hand to the lifeguard shrouded in a huge towel; he had small regard for these early-bird swimmers. But Nancy was ecstatic. Her spirits lifted with excitement. Not about anything specific, she told herself. Just a joyous anticipation of what would come next.

The water was perfect, just warm enough, with a tang of coolness left from the rain. She struck out strongly, remembering how she had resisted being taught to swim until she was twelve, and then, in one short summer, had abandoned her mud crawling, even learning to dive that year. Girls were funny creatures, she decided, rolling over to backstroke to the beach.

The sun was warm upon her face, the water slid like silk along her limbs. Long experience told her when she was near the shore and could turn, drop her feet, and —

And see Eric there, waving to her. She rubbed the water from her face and walked toward him, laughing because of the way he was dressed. Always completely conservative, that morning he was wearing a red shirt, checkered slacks, red and black, and a green canvas hat pulled down to shade his eyes from the sun behind her.

"I want to talk to you, Nancy," he was saying.

"What about my swim?"

"This is important . . ."

"All right." She waded out, and let him fold her short robe about her shoulders. "Can you risk ruining that costume to sit on the sand?" she asked.

He laughed. "My family keep giving me presents," he explained. "I've packed my clothes . . ."

"Well, I don't know if I call those things *clothes,* either. What was it you wanted to talk about?"

He sat facing her, his eyes in shadow because of the hat brim. "I want to ask you," he said quietly, "if you will go to England with me."

She gasped. Though, last night, Tim had said . . .

"But you're not serious!" she told Eric.

"Oh, yes! I told you last night — at dinner at your house that I was going. The people over there said they still wanted me."

"But of course they do!"

"Well, I wasn't sure. But it *is* work I want to do. And once — at some time — you seemed so interested in the work I'll do . . ."

"I am interested, Eric. You're a fine surgeon, and your ideas for research — It's all most exciting, and I envy you the things you will do, the people you'll work with —

"I believe my first project is going to be the ganglia of the neck, Nancy. You know how crippling a compression of those vertebrae can be! People make jokes about whiplash, but a genuine injury can be pure hell. That close to the brain, an injured axis is nothing to be handled by a heavy-handed, though well-meaning, surgeon. I've heard myself advising no recourse to surgery to such victims. Yet there must be a way to do surgery, or at least to train surgeons in that technique alone with a minimal risk of paralysis . . ."

She listened with genuine interest and sympathy, forgetting the time . . .

"I'm glad you're going to go and do your

research," she told Eric warmly. "You had me worried that day when exam reports came in, though I should have known you would not accept the setback —"

"I was accepting it that day."

"Oh, we all have times of disappointment, and we feel that life cannot possibly ever be good again —"

"Do you, Nancy? Have such times?"

"Well, of course! How do you think I felt when I found myself in jail just because I'd been interested in poor Amy and had tried to be kind to her?"

"That was a major foul-up, all right."

"Yes, it certainly was. But it cleared itself up, and your discouragement melted, too. You'll do great work in London, and do well with your life."

"I'd do better if I had you with me."

She shook her head and leaned forward to look at the watch on his wrist. "I have to be at the courthouse at nine," she explained. "You don't need me, Eric . . ."

"Oh, yes, I do. You have a way of giving me confidence. You never did feel that my failure to make diplomate was fatal to my career. You've backed me up for many years, and in many ways. We've been buddies as long as I can remember, and we'd do great things together on my new job."

264

Nancy nodded. "And Gayle would just be thrilled to death to have me tag along with you two . . ."

He reached for her arm and held it strongly. "Shut up, will you?" he asked. "Gayle is not going to England with me."

Nancy stared at him. "She really isn't?"

"Nup. She gave my ring back two nights ago."

On Saturday night?

"Was that what you two were doing while I was being arrested?"

He laughed. "It didn't happen just that way. But, yes, she decided that I was not going to be a big-wheel doctor; I told her definitely that I would not give up medicine and ever manage the hotel . . . Now she says she is going to do that."

"That's just talk. Even she knows she's too young for such a job."

"She thinks not. She thinks, with Grampa's help and backing, she can swing it. The Parmeleys agree, and I would vote that way, myself."

"What about Barbara?"

"What about her? She's only sixteen. Maybe in another ten years she could begin to learn."

"From Gayle?"

"Why not?"

Nancy shrugged. "Was it to manage the hotel she gave your ring back?"

"No, that idea hit her just last night. She gave the ring back after Amy died, and she knew — I suppose she realized that Tim would now be free . . ."

Nancy swallowed the retort on her tongue. She reached for her canvas shoes.

"Though what she does in that direction, Nancy," Eric was saying, "really doesn't matter. I am asking *you* to go to England with me."

She stared at him. "But to work, not . . ."

"Yes, that is what I mean. I really do love you, Nancy. I've been fond of you for years, and I know I can trust you. Gayle always said you were in love with me . . . ?" Now he was looking at her anxiously.

Nancy shook sand out of the shoes, and felt a shiver run along her skin. Eric. This was what she had wanted, this was a part of a dream. She looked up into his face, into his steady blue eyes.

"I'm not just jumping from one girl to another," he said, still anxiously.

She got to her knees, leaned over and kissed him, salt tingling on her lips. "I know you're not, Eric, dear," she said. "And I have been in love with you. It gave me wonderful thoughts and dreams. But now —"

"What about now?" he asked. "Oh, maybe I don't blame you . . ."

"But I am to blame," she said serenely. "Because I'm the one who has fallen really in love with another man."

He stared at her numbly.

She nodded. "I am going to marry Tim Dineen," she said. "I don't know when. But right now, this minute, I know what it is to love a man. And we shall be married." He had not asked her. Not really. But she sat in a rosy, warm glow of happy certainty that she would be Tim's wife, and —

She glanced at Eric, able to read the emotions which crossed his face. She had surprised him, and, yes, even shocked him. He gazed at her in disbelief, but able, in his turn, to read her thoughts. He took a deep breath and nodded acceptance.

"Boy," he breathed, "did I ever miss the boat!"

Nancy smiled. "Yes. You did," she agreed. "Even a month ago, I would have gone with you, as happy as a lark, and the whole thing might have worked out just fine. Because then I thought, as you did, that Tim belonged to Gayle. I was actually shocked when she said you two were marrying. I never did think you would."

"Was that what I did, turn you to Tim?"

"Oh, no. Tim did everything for himself."

"Yeah. He would. He's a great guy, Nancy."

She smiled and stood up. He rose, too.

"I feel sure I wish you happiness, Nancy," he said. "And I'll mean it, too, after I figure my real part in all this. And let's not mention Gayle again."

"I won't," she promised. "She's getting what she thinks she wants. She's probably already busy up there." She gestured toward the hotel. She took a few steps toward home. "You've really done nothing, Eric," she said. "Not even that red shirt and your hat made any difference. I'm still very fond of you."

He nodded. "Yeah. Thanks. I guess. And you have my blessing. I guess. Though I still cannot believe that you and Tim . . ."

"Ask him," she said. "He believes it. And that's what counts."

"Yes. Of course it is."

She looked back at the sea. Streaks of rosy pink tipped the in-rolling surf, the whole eastern sky was rosy pink. "I have to run," she said. "I'll see you again before I leave, before you do. But — good luck, Eric, darling."

He grinned. "I'll have what luck is left over," he said.

"It will be enough ! You'll find another —

268

what was it you called me? A boat?"
Laughter sparkled in her voice. "You'll find
another one." She ran up the beach; he
watched her disappear around the corner of
the hotel.

Then he glanced back at the water. "No
boat in sight," he grumbled.

Chapter 14

"Could I persuade you to make rounds with my family, Mrs. Dineen?" asked the surgeon, stripping off his gloves, shaking his chin free of the mask.

"I'll settle for a cup of coffee with the Staff," said his assistant, almost completely enshrouded in her gray-green robe and cap and mask.

"The Staff doesn't have time to dally with the girls."

"A likely story!" said Nancy, her eyes dancing.

The nurse who came to assist the doctor smiled at them both. All three were watching through the open door as the patient was wheeled off to Recovery.

"Nice job, Doctor," said the nurse.

"Thank you, Miss Martin. Will *you* have time for coffee?"

"Always remembering that doctor has a jealous wife!" warned the assistant, emerging from her gown, her cap, and her mask.

The three laughed. The nurse picked up the gloves and other gear lying around scrub. She enjoyed the Dineens. Married three years, they still constantly showed how much in love they were.

"Nancy's a lucky girl," she told the orderly who came for the hamper.

"He's the lucky one. She married him, and still works for big money."

"I heard she was quitting."

"Leave. Maternity, maybe, you think?"

"I think that would be very nice."

It was very nice. Both Tim and Nancy thought so. "I deplore the good sense that made us wait three years to have you and the rabbit get together," Tim told his wife as they each tasted the coffee, and made faces about it.

"I think our nice, gray-shingled house *and* a few dollars in the bank will impress our child with our readiness to take adequate care of him," said Nancy. "What if Powell says no?" she asked.

"Then, back to the drawing board, I suppose." He was grinning, and she blushed obligingly.

"He'll say yes," Tim told her, standing up. "When do you see him?"

"Any time today that o.r. doesn't need me. He said to 'run over.' "

"Well, watch that running. Catch me on the bleeper when you have news."

"I will, dear. Don't you be too rough on the new residents."

"Who? Me? I'm known as Pussycat Dineen in all the dayrooms."

She laughed and watched him as he went out into the hall. Tall, sure of himself, kind — able —

"I married a great guy," she told herself.

She looked at her schedule, and decided that the best course to follow would be to call ob. and see if Dr. Powell could see her right away, then get back to surgery . . .

As she went down the hall, she could see Tim at the far end of it, a dozen white-coated young men and three women in a semicircle around him. His Family. "They think he's wonderful, too," she told herself contentedly.

As she waited for the elevator, she watched him. He had pulled a lab coat over his scrub suit, and stood listening, talking — teaching — those around him. She nodded. Yes! It was a good thing, their marriage.

Dr. Dineen had seen his wife at the elevator, but he continued his questions, his listening to the answers, his comments.

His Family consisted of four residents, somewhat new to his service, seven interns, four of them rotating, and two women interns, assigned for the first time to surgery.

The doctor — the Staff, as he was designated — welcomed these two warmly. "Orthopedics is supposed to be a lesser-traumatic experience than some surgical departments," he said. "But don't count on it, ladies. Do not count on it. Also, try to accustom yourselves to the fact that I shall most certainly call a group of learning doctors 'men'. This is a wordy profession, and I economize where possible. Now! Shall we proceed?"

They trailed the doctor a short distance down the hall. He led the way to the bedside of a black woman who observed the advancing parade. She rejoiced in two lovely shiners. One leg was elevated in a traction apparatus.

Dr. Dineen glanced at his chart board, and then his eyes selected one of the residents. "Dr. Evans," he said.

A tall, rangy redhead shifted his shoulders. "Mrs. Benear . . ." he began.

"Mostly folks call me by my first name," said the woman on the bed. "Mine's Pauline." Her eyes alertly watching the young doctor.

He did not falter. "Mrs. Benear," he said firmly, "was last Friday the victim of a purse snatching. She defended herself, was knocked down, resulting in a fracture of the femur and a contusion of the scalp. Some concussion which seems to be clearing. The fracture . . ."

"He talk real good!" said the patient to Tim as the group moved on.

"Yes, he does," said the doctor warmly. "Has your husband seen your black eyes?"

"He sure has, Doctor! He say he couldn't done better hisself!"

Tim chuckled and listened to the report on the first of the ward patients.

"We seem to have lost a couple," he said, flipping over pages on his board.

He called on one of the women for a report on the first of these. Her voice trembled a little as she started. Mr. D'Aquila had died early on Sunday morning. "His blood pressure kept dropping, and dropping . . ."

"Measures, Doctor?" asked Tim.

"Yes, sir. Transfusions . . ." She specified amounts and type. "But . . ." she shrugged, "he just shuffled off without any particular terminal incident."

A couple of the doctors laughed. Dr. Dineen turned to look at her. "Er — yes," he agreed. "I see. Will you see that I get a report on the autopsy, Doctor?"

"Yes, sir," said the intern, her confidence by then returning.

The next name, too, was that of a man who had had hip socket replacement surgery ten days before. And who had died.

Dr. Dineen selected a third-year resident to make that report, pointing out this doctor's status to the others. "Which doesn't mean he always knows what he is talking about," he concluded, seeming to be intent on what he was writing on his chart board. "Dr. Hemmer?"

The resident was not perturbed. He made a concise résumé of the case. "The patient," he said, "had had a lousy postop course." He serenely met Dr. Dineen's lifted eyes.

"Okay," Tim agreed. "I'll accept *lousy*. These things make for good reading in a staff meeting. Go on, Hemmer."

"Yes, sir. Well, as you know . . ."

"I know what I need to know," snapped Dr. Dineen. "Make your report to all of us."

"Yes, *sir!* The patient developed a clot in the femoral artery, and threw an embolus — a big one — from it to his lung, and on Sunday afternoon went out like a light. Yesterday. Staff was notified."

Tim nodded. "I was here," he agreed. "Our department had a big weekend. Now . . ."

"Telephone, Dr. Dineen," said a nurse at the door.

Tim nodded. It would be Nancy. "Wait in the hall," he told his Family, and strode out of the ward.

Behind him he heard Dr. Hemmer explaining that the hip socket surgery had taken ten hours and the Chief was really great!

Tim spoke eagerly into the telephone. The caller was not Nancy. He drummed his fingers on the desk top.

It was two hours later that he caught up with Nancy. She was in o.r., winding up a case. He held a mask to his face and went inside. Her eyes smiled to see him.

He looked at the patient and said, "Lunch?" to his wife.

She nodded. "Sure. Will you pay?"

"Sure. Ten minutes?"

"Make it half an hour."

"My insides are rattling . . ."

"I'll try to hurry."

Maybe she did hurry. And then had to hunt for Tim in the X-ray viewing room. "Come along," she said from the door. "I have a class in less than an hour."

He snapped off the lights and joined her. "Sounds like corned beef sandwiches," he said.

She shrugged.

"What's this I heard about your wanting

to train surgical assistants for Emergency Receiving?"

"A-huh. Oh, the training won't be too different . . ."

"But they will need to know karate down there. That place is *wild!*"

She laughed and went into the elevator which already held a stretcher and the patient's attendants.

When the Gurney was moved out, she and Tim both spoke at once, saying almost the same thing.

"I had an urgent call from Gayle."

They gazed at each other, then went across the hall to the cafeteria where they picked up their trays and started down the line.

Nancy chose a salad, Tim a bowl of soup.

"It slops," she warned him.

"Not with my steady hand."

"Humph! There aren't any corned beef sandwiches."

"What on earth will we *do?*"

She decided on chicken, and put a ham and cheese on his tray.

"Henpecked," he muttered, deciding on a baked apple.

"That looks good."

"So do the sliced peaches."

She took the peaches; they picked up

milk, and Tim signed the check. Nancy went on to claim a small table next to the wall.

"Why do we have pink-flowered wallpaper on these walls?" Tim asked, unloading his tray.

"It's supposed to be cheerful for us hardworking personnel."

"Doesn't always cheer me up."

"I know." She brushed her cap back off her head, the fine golden hair wisping. Tim's forefinger touched one of these locks.

"You're tired."

"Doesn't that go with lunch? Gayle said we would *have* to come."

"She tell you why? What has happened?"

"No, just said that she needed us."

Tim finished his soup, and set the bowl to one side. He reached for lettuce from Nancy's salad. "What *happened*," he said, "is that Gayle is asking us for help. I never thought I'd see the day."

"You look like a rabbit with lettuce hanging down your chin. Did you say you'd go?"

"Rabbits don't have chins. No. I told her I couldn't possibly get away. I have two bone grafts and a fusion."

"I know you do. Want half my sandwich?"

"Sure. We'll swap halves."

"I have a completely full schedule myself, Tim."

"Did you tell her that?"

"I did. She didn't seem to think it made any difference."

He nodded. Then stood up because another doctor had brought his tray to their table. From then on the talk was pure shop, with each of the Dineens watching the clock.

They were finished with the meal and were waiting for the elevator when Tim grabbed Nancy's arm. "Hey!" he cried, "you didn't tell me what Powell had to say."

"Oh!" She was as surprised as he to realize . . . "I forgot. We —"

"I know. Corned beef sandwiches, and bone grafts, and Gayle. Important things. But what did the guy *say?*"

"He said that it was a good thing we bought a house with two extra bedrooms. That we'd need one of 'em for diaper pails and stuff as of next May."

The elevator came, people got off. But Tim stood where he was, his hands on her shoulders. His eyes were smiling. "Nancy," he said deeply, "you're wonderful!"

"Oh, I don't think I want to be called wonderful," she said airily. "Nice, maybe. Good. Reliable. But I wouldn't want to try to live up to *wonderful.*"

"All right," he agreed readily. "I'll change it to adequate."

Then her smiles broke through. "I'll try 'wonderful' on for size," she agreed. "Oh, Tim . . ."

"Great, isn't it?" he agreed. "Where the hell is that elevator?"

"We let one come and go."

"Acting like fool parents, huh?"

"It's only the beginning. Do we ever have plans to make!"

"You're to stop work."

"By the first of the year."

"We'll see. Did you tell Gayle?"

"She wouldn't have listened. She was so full of her own affairs."

"But yours had to be more important. What about your mother?"

"When we go there for our weekend." They did go to the Beach, every fourth weekend. "I'll knit bootees or something."

Tim chuckled.

"I think Gayle wanted us right away."

"Can't possibly," said Tim, letting her precede him to the empty elevator. "Whatever she wants, it's not our specialty."

"Hotel management, you mean?"

"I mean I can't go. And —"

"I can't either. I told her so. I told her I'd

280

be of no help. And she said that we'd know the right person to get to help her."

Tim bent over to look at his wife. "Does that mean something?"

Nancy shrugged. "I expect I'll talk to her again this evening. But I still can't get away before Saturday."

They said they would not go to the Beach.

They each did go.

Knowing that the other would.

Because when Nancy called her sister that evening — Tim had a staff conference meeting and would not be at home for diner. It was on such occasions that their professions could fail closely to parallel each other.

Nancy, having reached their gray shingled town house, and admired again the diamond-panel windows, the pink geraniums on the stoop, and knew the quiet satisfaction of having their own home, picked up the telephone and got through to Gayle.

Who did seem terribly upset.

"Listen to me, Gayle," said Nancy firmly. "You have to tell me exactly —"

"I can't talk about it. We don't want the word spreading."

"But if you don't tell me . . ."

"I will tell you when you come. But through the switchboard . . ."

★ ★ ★

Nancy spent a busy evening, and was in bed when Tim came home. She let him try not to disturb her, and lay there, listening to him as he did the routine bedtime things; he set out fresh clothes, put his used things neatly away in hamper and closet.

But when he turned off the bathroom light and got into bed, leaning over lightly to kiss her, she said, "Gayle says they may have bubonic plague at the hotel."

She felt the whole bed shake under his surprise. And she laughed a little.

"That's complete nonsense!" he said. "What's she trying to do now?"

"She wants us to come to the Beach."

"Did you tell her we couldn't do that?"

"Yes. She wouldn't talk much, just kept saying the hotel had been stricken."

He slid his arm under her shoulders. "Tell her to send for Eric. He can get home as quickly as I can get away. For now, let's go to sleep. We have to take care of ourselves if we're having a baby."

She smiled. "Oh, we're having one."

Within minutes, he did go to sleep, but Nancy lay wide-eyed awake. The ruffles of the crisscross organdy curtains, because of that lamp down at the front door, made patterns on the ceiling. Tim's breathing came steadily, strongly.

And Nancy thought. About he call she had made that evening to Gayle at the hotel. She could remember each thing Gayle had said. She could picture Gayle . . .

She couldn't talk through the switchboard, she had said again.

"Then go to an outside phone and call me."

Gayle did that, which marked the seriousness of her problem. She was not one to take orders from anyone, least of all Nancy.

But that night she went to a lobby booth and called Nancy within five minutes, which meant she had not stopped to exchange any chitchat with people in the lobby. That also indicated the seriousness of her problem.

"I want you to come," she said again. "The hotel has been stricken . . ."

"Oh, now, Gayle . . ."

"It has been, Nancy. Something has stricken our guests. Even some of the help . . ."

"Stricken in what way, Gayle?"

"Nausea, diarrhea — cramps."

"What does the doctor say?"

"He's stricken, too, and he thinks it's food poisoning or some terrible infection like bubonic plague."

Nancy had also called this nonsense.

"He told me to cancel reservations," said Gayle soberly, "until we *know*. I have two conventions coming in next Sunday and Monday."

That was serious, Nancy knew.

"What have you done?"

"I called you and Tim. It started last night . . . If it is something like the plague, Nancy, and the Government comes in, they'd close us down. It could ruin us."

"It does sound serious."

"I've done everything I could think of. In the kitchen, the dining areas . . . Things seem clean, the food is cared for as we always do. We have an A rating. And of course we are trying to keep the problem hushed up . . ."

"Have you talked to the hospital people?"

"I may have to do that. But I had hoped to keep this quiet . . ."

"I don't see how you can. Food poisoning can kill people, Gayle!"

"I know," said Gayle mournfully. "I wish someone would come. I even called Eric — when you two so flatly turned me down. But — Please do come!"

"Tim can't. He has important surgery tomorrow." Surgery he wanted to do. Bone grafts were regularly being brought to his skilled hands from distances away. Though this would not impress Gayle in her time of trouble. "And Eric is so far away."

"He could get here overnight, if he wanted to come."

Yes. He could.

Nancy said again that Gayle should get in professional help. That Tim could not come. If she found time, she might . . . "But I don't think I'd be any real help."

Lying there against Tim's shoulder, she thought that she might have driven to the Beach that evening, while Tim was gone, and found out for herself what was happening. Food poisoning — the hotel surely would refrigerate custards, obvious things like that. Meats . . . They certainly would check on any canned goods being used . . . The city water was regularly checked . . .

She could, maybe, drive down tomorrow. Get away from the hospital the minute she was free, leaving word for Tim. She was not scheduled for his o.r., except for a laminectomy in the morning. Yes, possibly she could work it in.

But, darn it, why did Gayle have to interfere? She seemed much more concerned with hushing the thing up than in controlling its cause! Nancy could just imagine the hotel. The scurrying about behind scenes, the air of bland imperturbability before the guests.

She began to plan her drive down to the Beach the next afternoon. She might even get in a swim —

She turned on her side, ready to go to sleep.

Gayle had interfered, but she couldn't, really, disturb Nancy's life. Here she and Tim were, married — for just about three years, now. Last spring they had bought this house and furnished it. Now they were ready to start a family. All good things, from their point of view. Nancy would give up her work, care for her home, market and clean, and take care of her husband and child. Children. And if Gayle got into tricky situations — which she seemed to have done —

Gayle had indeed telephoned overseas to Eric Ritter. She caught him at a bad time. In fact, when her call came through, it was already evening in London, with a light rain falling and the perfume of some flowering shrubs in the air. Eric had invited a young woman to have dinner with him in his flat. He really was interested in the girl; she came of a good family, and was lovely to look at, with silky hair which reminded him of Nancy Colburn, and truly English porcelain skin, a well-modulated voice —

She was modern enough, and did research work in a barrister's office in the Temple. Eric had been able to make her laugh by telling her about the new surgeon he was working with recently.

"I'd just about got used to the other man's idiosyncrasies . . ."

Oh, yes, he was entirely capable, but he was a conceited sort of chap. "In the States we'd call him snooty. But this fellow, this new one, is spooky."

He had to define that term, too. "At first he seemed quite pleasant and personable, but today I decided that he was sarcastic and very opinionated."

"And you're not?" Iris had teased.

"Oh, yes, I daresay I am." In his three years in London, Eric had learned to say things like "daresay" instead of "guess" or "suppose." "But I don't lecture the way this chap does. For example, this morning, one of our students had the bad luck to mention an article on kneecap replacement in an American magazine. And our doctor-preceptor took off on a half-hour harangue on the practice — American, of course — of printing pseudo-scientific articles as fact in popular publications. This of course let him slide into a delineation of his opinions on almost anything American. This ranged from our President in office to the way we spell — *misspell* — words like honor and favor, and such."

"Aren't your American magazines pretty well authenticated when they publish scientific articles?"

He was prepared to say they were, indeed, but at that precise moment, the overseas operator spoiled everything. And Gayle again stepped into his life.

Because of his grandfather, the call itself frightened him. Once it was established that Grampa was all right, he listened to what Gayle was saying.

The call so vividly recalled home to his mind that, afterward, he found himself talking freely, even excitedly, to Iris about the beach and the hotel.

She was interested in all that he told, and encouraged him to elaborate. She asked about "this Gayle," and of course that brought in other things. He mentioned Nancy —

"You were in love with her!"

"Oh, yes. Though for a short, hectic time I thought I was in love with Gayle."

"No longer?"

"Not with Gayle, no."

For the minute he was transported from the softly lighted sitting room of his London flat, the misty air beyond the open windows, the rich, dim colors of wax-polished oak and old velvet furnishings to the sun-washed beach, the bright flags, the gaiety and movement of the hotel terrace —

"Couldn't you go?" Iris asked him intently.

He blinked and considered what she had asked. "I could," he agreed.

"This woman, this Gayle, if she has accepted responsibility for the hotel and its operation, I should think . . ."

"That we owe her something in return. Yes — we may —"

She smiled at him.

"Would you go with me?" Eric asked.

Her eyebrows lifted. "Will you be there long?"

"I don't believe I can manage more than a day or so."

"Then I shall risk letting you go alone."

Eric said nothing of his reasons for not wanting to go back to the Beach, to Gayle, and to his family. He had so recently begun to feel that he was free of his obligations to those things, free to do his work, and to build, carefully, new relationships, a new life . . .

But he did the necessary telephoning and made the necessary adjustments; he packed a bag, and the next morning taxied to Heathrow. He would just see what the trouble was. See his grandfather, and give such advice as seemed to be his to give.

Nancy, finished with her scheduled duties, asked permission to leave by three that afternoon. She wrote a brief note to Tim, who was in conference over at another building of the complex, she went out to her car and drove east. To see what really was going on at Peter's Beach.

Like Eric, she was remembering the hotel, what it had meant to her personally, what it meant to their part of the country. It would be a shame to let such an institution die for want of a little advice.

"I can't *do* anything," she told herself. "But maybe I can suggest means and places where Gayle can find real help. I'll see Grampa and talk to him. She may be trying to keep this crisis from him. He'd probably know exactly what to do!"

As for Tim, during the final stages of his conference, which dealt with administrative matters, he began to wonder where Nancy was, what she was doing — and if, maybe, he could not find time and opportunity to run out to the Beach to discover just exactly what in hell Gayle had let happen at the hotel! He did not want Nancy troubled.

And so they gathered. And so they came together on the mezzanine of the hotel, in the corridor, and in Gayle's office.

Nancy in her trim skirt and blouse, her hair drawn back, tied with a scarf that matched the blouse. Gayle wore a linen suit — slacks, coat, black and white dotted scarf.

Next came Eric, looking quite different from the way they remembered him. His light-wool suit was perfectly tailored, his hair was full but trim against the thin line of white shirt collar that was showing. His manner of speaking was clipped, his collo-quialisms were not local . . .

"You've gone Limey!" Tim accused him, when he came bounding up the stairs, dark red pull-on shirt and gray plaid slacks.

They laughed to see each other; they were glad to see each other; they all talked at once —

But Gayle was so obviously distraught, worried, and threatening to get panicky that they soon settled down. It was Nancy who in-sisted that Grampa be in on their conference.

"Oh, Nancy —"

"He hasn't been told. I thought not."

"But —"

"He's old, and this will upset him. But I'll go get him."

This she did, and Gayle was forced to tell them all exactly what had happened. For three days, she said, people in the hotel had been getting ill. Not all the people, not only guests . . . but quite a few were sick. Six. Ten, perhaps. Suddenly, and rather severely. Cramps, nausea, diarrhea . . .

In the middle of her story, Tim let himself correct her sharply when she used the word *nauseous* instead of *nauseated*. "You sound like a comedian on TV," he said. "Using what I call nicely, nicely English. They became nauseated. We are here to discover the nauseous condition in your hotel."

"All right, all right!" said Gayle. "Just get to work and find out what's wrong, and what we'll do about it!"

"There must be a solution," said Grampa slowly. "Other than closing. We may have to close the dining rooms . . ."

"Could you bring food in from outside?" asked Tim. "There are catering firms in the city . . ."

Yes, that could be done. It would be terribly expensive, said Gayle, and was silenced swiftly and completely.

Had she talked to the hospital pathologists? What about Public Health?

She had made every effort to keep the trouble quiet.

She was rebuked for this. An open statement would be vastly preferable to proliferating gossip and surmise.

Then she told of one guest who had insisted on going to the hospital, and the pathologist there had warned Gayle that he had found salmonella. Of course it might be from something the woman had eaten away from the hotel, but the hotel should be alert.

That was when she had called in the family. Grampa was indignant that she had not told him. The others hinted, then said outright, that it would be good for Gayle to know she could need help.

Again, and meekly, she urged them to *do* something.

Grampa mentioned the Grade A rating of the hotel's food service, which they prided themselves on maintaining. Their water supply was the town's, and it was approved. What about milk?

A couple of phone calls certified its quality. The hospital had had no cases, and they used the same service.

"I don't really think it is bubonic plague," Tim drawled.

This startled Eric. "Who said . . . ?"

This put Gayle on the spot again, and

Nancy felt sorry for her.

She called the group to order, and said that time was short. Yes, for each of them, but mainly for the hotel and its food service. Public Health must be notified.

Meanwhile, they should do some constructive thinking. Custards and canned goods were always suspect. Ground meat. Canned mushrooms had been known to cause trouble. Yes, and there was a case where green beans . . .

"We use fresh ones," said Gayle. "Fresh vegetables, always."

"What about fish? Your meat surely is inspected, but you serve quantities of fish . . ."

Eric said they should go back to the very first case of distress. Would they have any record of what was served each day, what eaten, by individual guests?

Nancy mentioned that he said re-*cord* in the English way, and he smiled at her. "I want a good chance to *talk* to you," she whispered.

"I can hear you," Tim warned her.

Grampa was assuring them that individual tickets from the guests' meals would be on file. And he surely would hope that each kitchen would have daily lists of food prepared and served. He'd hope that!

Gayle flushed and said that no orders to

the contrary had ever been given.

Grampa nodded. "But we have no way of knowing what guests eat elsewhere," he reminded the young people.

They looked at him with respect.

"The first thing to do is to be sure our kitchens are clean, our food well cared for . . ."

The thing then to do, after calling Public Health and knowing that an inspector would be there in the morning, would be to make an inspection for themselves.

"But we shouldn't change anything," said Nancy.

At least four people explained why to Gayle. "You're still trying to sweep our trouble under the rug," Eric told her angrily.

Grampa said he'd just be a handicap, would slow them down, because of the wheelchair. Nancy said that could be managed nicely. Unless they should fan out and make the inspections singly and more quickly?

No, they would go together, get the advantage of each other's experience and suggestions. It made a notable parade. But it progressed through each kitchen and pantry, to supply rooms. Grampa could tell them that the kitchens and serving areas were steam-cleaned once a year. They were each in turn closed down for twenty-four hours . . . Gayle said the exact dates of the last cleaning would be in her office.

So, upstairs they went again. And after a little more talk, Tim said he must get back to his hospital. "I am doing more and more ortho-neurosurgery," he told Eric. "Those cases take a lot of postop care."

"Yes, they do. I'll try to stop to see you before I leave."

"I certainly hope so!"

"Tonight I'll talk to Grampa for a little, then get to bed. I suspect I've lost a night's sleep somewhere."

"Jet lag," said Gayle importantly. "Will you fellows be back when the Public Health man comes?"

The men looked at Nancy, they looked at each other. "Nancy can talk to him," said Tim. "She can spend the night with her parents, and be here tomorrow to talk and to listen."

"I could do that much!" said Gayle.

"I don't think so. This will take more than a pretty face and a sexy body."

"Well, thank you so much!" said Nancy briskly.

Tim stood up, he bent over and lightly kissed her. But the shine in his eyes said all the things that he had already said to her, and would say again.

Gayle watched them.

"You'd better attend to getting that catered food service into operation," Eric told her. "I'll put Grampa to bed."

The whole story had to be told to the Colburns. Nancy was ready for bed when that time finally came. And the next morning Mrs. Colburn was ready to go back to the hotel with her.

"But, Mother . . ."

"I don't want to lose any time with you."

"I'll be busy."

"I'll try to keep up with you, and out of the way, too. Besides, I want to see Gayle."

So Veronica Colburn went to the hotel, and said she would accompany Nancy as she "looked around." She did follow her, agreeing that the trouble must be with the food. "Our water supply is good, so if the plumbing is in shape . . ."

Nancy made a note on the chart board which she carried. She had asked for and got the health records of all food-handling employees.

Mrs. Colburn had never seen the hotel kitchens. The long, stainless steel counters, the racks and racks of pots and pans, spoons and ladles, the knives — the stoves — the refrigerators. After a glance for permission, she opened doors, like a child in a toystore.

"We have a new chef," Gayle told her. "He personally goes to market for his supplies."

"Look at the eggs!" cried Mrs. Colburn, standing before one open refrigerator. "But — *Nancy!* Will you look here?"

Nancy turned back from the freezer room which she was about to enter. She looked over her mother's ample shoulder. "Eggs," she said.

"Well, of course they're eggs!"

Eggs were certainly there. Trays and trays of eggs, as well as mesh containers of more eggs, jumbled into the square baskets.

"What's up?" asked Eric, coming in. Mrs. Colburn exclaimed and he kissed her.

"Mom's looking at eggs," said Nancy. "Did you sleep well, Eric?"

"Like a top. I believe one needs a hotel and its noises . . ." He broke off to look keenly at Mrs. Colburn, who was taking eggs from one of the baskets and bringing them to a bright, spotless table.

"See there!" she said.

The three young people leaned forward. Eric reached for an egg. "This one is cracked," he said.

"They are all cracked!" cried Mrs.

Colburn. "And there's your first clue, Miss Gayle!"

"Cracked eggs?" she said, not believing.

But Nancy and Eric were looking in awe at the eggs, at Nancy's mother, at each other.

"That would do it!" said Eric.

"Why would they have baskets and baskets of cracked eggs?" Nancy asked. "Of course to save money — pennies. But that's ridiculous! Eggs don't cost that much!"

"Did you say you had a new chef," she asked Gayle, "who does your food shopping?"

"Ye-es."

"Can you get him here?"

"Of course, but —" She went to the house phone, and the chef arrived within minutes. The whole kitchen staff must have been anxiously awaiting summons.

The new chef was a rather young man, immaculately clean. Yes, he said, he bought eggs for the hotel kitchens. He explained that he went to market himself, and bought wisely. Meat, vegetables — everything as good and as cheap as he could. He was hoping to establish himself in this big, fine hotel. He rolled an eye at Gayle.

"Do you buy *cracked* eggs?" asked Nancy, her voice firm.

"But certainly, miss. They are bargains, they are fresh and do well for cooking, thickening, sauces — scrambled eggs. It keeps the food costs down."

Unless one ran into a batch of contaminated . . .

Nancy and Eric stared at each other, and they stared at Mrs. Colburn.

"As simple as that!" said Nancy in hushed awe. Then she laughed; Eric joined her, and Mrs. Colburn. They tried to explain to the chef, and to Gayle, how bacteria could enter a cracked egg. It wouldn't take much. And they laughed again.

Though Gayle was furious. The chef should have known! Yes, he should have. And whoever was above him in the food operation.

"Well," she declared, "at least now we know how and what to *do!* We just won't serve any eggs!"

"You can't do that!" cried Nancy. She and Eric and the chef were dragging the bulk-egg baskets out of the refrigerator. The chef was almost in tears of contrition and apology.

"We won't serve these eggs!" he assured Mrs. Colburn.

But the mystery was solved. The Public

Health man arrived, and agreed that their problem was already behind them. "Though I'd still steam-clean that refrigerator — maybe this whole kitchen. You're very lucky," he told the hotel manager, "to have the assistance of a good housekeeper."

"And there was only a little publicity," said Grampa, who, like Gayle, was not very amused.

"And no fatality," said the P.H. man, ready to make out his report. "Some guests knew discomfort, maybe an employee or two?"

Yes, that was the case.

"There was danger to many, however," he addressed himself sternly to Gayle. "In the future . . ."

"She is learning," said Grampa.

Nancy called Tim and told him what had transpired. He, too, laughed and said he would be over to fetch Nancy. She was to let Eric use her car.

"He's moaning over the plane fare he spent."

"I bleed for him. Kiss your mother for me. She saved more lives than we doctors do."

This pleased Veronica, who said she wanted to go home and cook dinner for them all.

"I do hope this will solve Gayle's whole problem," she said earnestly. "This hotel management is the first thing in her life that the girl has ever stuck with. I *want* it to be a success for her sake and ours. Your father and I won't feel that we've failed with her. In raising her, I mean, Nancy."

"I know what you mean, mother. And I am beginning to understand what a task raising a child can be. Much bigger than learning to be a nurse or a housekeeper."

"You're those things already, aren't you?" her mother asked.

"I've learned the nursing, yes," said Nancy. "But not the housekeeping . . . not really. Though I plan to study hard on that while I'm expecting the baby."

Everyone turned sharply to look at her. "What baby?" asked Mrs. Colburn blankly, then she understood, and she reached her outstretched arms to Nancy. "You're only now *telling* me?" she cried.

There was quite a flurry of excitement. It persisted until late afternoon when they all gathered for Mrs. Colburn's dinner. "Without eggs?" asked Tim, coming in, his eyes searching for Nancy.

"Quite a celebration," he commented dryly, "over a matter of mass stupidity."

"Oh, we're celebrating Nancy's baby,"

said his father-in-law.

"That's going to be the last bash," drawled Gayle. "Nobody is ever going to top that."

"It might help us to forget the eggs," said Tim.

"I hope."

They were eating early. Eric was going back to the city with Nancy and Tim; he would catch a plane at nine the next morning.

"At least your journey was a success," said Mr. Colburn.

Eric looked at him in surprise. "Your wife was here to solve our problem, sir," he said. "I wasn't needed. Tim and Nancy were not."

"And the flush on our cheeks is not triumph," Tim agreed. "Though I really came to look at Gayle, who must finally be acknowledging that she could use our help."

"Oh, Tim!" Nancy protested.

"It's a lesson we all needed to learn," said Eric soberly. "That under all that beauty and *chic*, she still could stumble and almost fall . . ."

Gayle stood against the wall, wide-eyed. "Am I that sort of monster?" she asked.

Nancy smiled at her. "That sort of beautiful monster," she said softly. "I think I'll name my first daughter for you."

"Over my dead body!" cried Tim.

"Here, here!" said Eric.

We hope you have enjoyed this Large Print book. Other Thorndike Press or Chivers Press Large Print books are available at your library or directly from the publishers.

For more information about current and upcoming titles, please call or write, without obligation, to:

Thorndike Press
P.O. Box 159
Thorndike, Maine 04986 USA
Tel. (800) 257-5157

OR

Chivers Press Limited
Windsor Bridge Road
Bath BA2 3AX
England
Tel. (0225) 335336

All our Large Print titles are designed for easy reading, and all our books are made to last.